# MILLION MILES AWAY

## ALICE BANE

VisualBee
Publishing

Cover Design: Srjdan Filipovic
Photo Credit: 1. bezikus; www.shutterstock.com
            2. rybindmitriy; www.stock.adobe.com
Copyright ©2019 by Alice Bane
All rights reserved.
ISBN 978-1-989526-07-1

The characters and events portrayed in this book are fictitious or are used fictitiously. Any similarity to real persons, living or dead, is purely coincidental and not intended by the author.

VisualBee Publishing 2019
info@visualbeepublishing.com

Chapter
ONE

I focused on the sound my heels made on the paved sidewalk and made sure I was maintaining my pace. I clutched the handle of my sleek black briefcase, unintentionally digging my fingernails into the palm of my free hand. Glancing up, I noted a man in a business suit coming down the sidewalk in the opposite direction. I felt a sudden rush of anticipation as a smile formed on his lips.

"Anna!" he waved.

I exhaled the hopeful breath I held as a woman walking behind me pushed past and rushed into his arms. *Of course, he wasn't looking at me.* I bit my lip and walked faster, attempting to forget the sting of humiliation and hoped he hadn't noticed me.

I wasn't worried I would be late, nor was I rushing to see my coworkers. It was Laura's birthday and the three of us were planning on going out for drinks after work.

I groaned to myself. I love Laura and Abiola to death. They weren't just my assistants at work; they were so much more to me than that. But it was never fun to be the only sober person at the party, and for the past year, I hadn't had a drop of alcohol. This wasn't by choice; a while back, I developed a sleep disorder. Every night, I dreaded falling asleep, always petrified of what torments awaited me the moment I closed my eyes. Every few weeks I would suffer an episode of sleep paralysis, and every other night, I had to deal with bizarre nightmares.

As I approached the OSA building, I looked up and caught my breath. The sleek obsidian-like skyscraper towered over even the most formidable structures in its proximity. Las Vegas, a city once known only as a 24/7 celebration of debauchery and excess was now famous for being the home of OSA headquarters. While it was still possible to fulfill even the most twisted and depraved desires if one knew where to look, the drugs, prostitutes, violent sports, and other oddities had been forced underground; most of the time in a very literal sense.

Flyers and garbage no longer littered the streets. Crime, unemployment, and homelessness had all reached an all-time low and it was thanks, in part, to organizations connected with OSA. Over the past several decades, they established connections within every level of government. They had employed the most gifted individuals on the planet to reform the justice system, the prison system, health-care, welfare, and education. If there was a metaphorical pie on the table, they had a finger in it.

I stopped and took a moment to steady my nerves.

*You're going to go in there and be a good friend.* I told myself. *You're going to smile and say, "Happy 29th birthday." She's always there for you on your best and your worst days and you're going to make sure she knows how much she means to you. It doesn't matter how you feel about birthdays and being sober at a party.* I carefully fixed a few flyaway hairs. I had opted for a deeper red dye, hoping it would make up for the absolute bore I had become. Finally, I nodded at my reflection in the automatic doors then marched forward and entered the building.

"Welcome, Natalia," the facial recognition scanner greeted me.

"Thank you," I said, then shook my head irritably.

I always responded without thinking. I knew that it was only the building's A.I. doing what it was programmed to do, but it always felt wrong to not be polite to someone, or rather something, that was always polite to me. I stretched my neck and stood a little taller. I was in my element. In a lot of ways, this felt more like home than my house. I spend more waking hours here than I ever do at home anyway. And all my friends are here. OSA has been the one place where I always thrived. I have confidence that, with my talent and gumption, I'm unstoppable within these walls. Here, I'm a *goddess*.

Ever since I achieved Top-Rated status, I've done whatever it takes to keep the quality and quantity of the work I produce up to its maximum potential. After all, I didn't work my ass off for a scholarship to go to the best art school in the country to be anything less than extraordinary.

It was a great honor to be employed by OSA, or Our Space Association if you prefer to call it by its full name. But it's not as if I ended up there by accident. I give this place 110% of myself every single day. I willingly put in overtime on nights, holidays, and weekends. I never called in sick unless it's *really* serious, and I've never used a single vacation day in my entire adult life.

I made my way through the lobby, past the busy café and the gym, and walked up the first flight of stairs. Of course, I could have taken the escalator or the massive stainless-steel glass elevator, but taking the long way gave me a few extra minutes to myself. All the walls that separated the rooms on the bottom floors were made of glass. It made everything feel open and allowed everyone to take in just how huge the building was. There was no ceiling until you reached the third floor and even then, it was a vaulted dome with a projected image that changed daily.

That day, the dome projection was one of my most recent paintings depicting the Helix Nebula. I always had a special place in my heart for the Aquarius constellation that contained the iris-like Helix. Slightly creepy if you stared at it too long, but beautiful nonetheless. It's the closest to Earth of all the bright planetary nebulae and was the first I had ever seen as a child.

When I first got sick last year, I had gone through a brief phase where I drew human subjects, but the soft curves of the human face proved to be challenging. The faces I drew always seemed cold and angular no matter how much I practiced. It wasn't surprising that I gave up on that and opted to stick with what I was best at, which had always been astronomic rendering.

The first three floors of the OSA headquarters were dedicated to the enjoyment of its employees. The bottom floor contained a food court and a gym. The second floor housed a games room, a Zen garden, and a theater. The third floor had a spa, salon, and what everyone called the chill cave where you could utilize sleeping pods to take a nap at any point in your workday. OSA's doors were open around the clock, 365 a year. Management was less concerned with when its employees chose to work and more about their productivity. As long as you were completing the tasks assigned to you each week, you could set your own schedule, work at your own pace, and there were tons of perks at your fingertips anytime you needed a break.

This was another reason I excelled in that environment. I had always been a motivated person. On top of having a stellar work ethic, I discovered when I was in college that I had a unique gift for picking out images captured by OSA satellites and rendering them into works of art. My design instructor sent a digital painting of mine to his friend who was an OSA recruiter and I was offered a job fresh off the graduation stage. I soon became well-known within the company for my ability to combine one image with another and, through the manipulation of color and saturation, provoke strong emotions from those who viewed my work. Space had fascinated me since I was a little girl and delving into a detailed painting of a newly discovered astral body was a favorite escape of mine.

Abiola and Laura were the only people I felt any real connection with. High school had been such a nightmare that the moment I had the opportunity to reinvent myself, I disconnected from my old life. The person I was before I worked at OSA might as well have never existed. These women were a testament to the new life I had built since then; the dream job, the house, the body, the relationships. They were crucial pieces of the person I wanted to be, and I reminded myself that they deserved every bit of affection I could muster.

After climbing the six flights of stairs it took to reach the fourth floor, I huffed, eyeing the elevator doors. I walked up and pressed the smooth chrome button and awaited the glass chariot that would take me up to floor seven where I would spend the next nine hours of my day.

As soon as I walked into the art studio, I spotted Laura and Abiola who were already sitting at their stations giggling. Laura had a gigantic bouquet of roses from Alex and she was reading a poem that he had handwritten on the card.

"Alex is such a sweetheart. You better hang onto him," Abiola said with a playful pinch of Laura's arm.

Abiola was so exotic looking; curvy with mocha skin and Amber-colored eyes. She always wore her hair combed out into an afro. Her twist-outs were well defined and voluminous, swept back by a colorful headband that kept it all in check.

"I know," Laura replied and fanned herself coquettishly with the card. Her blonde wavy hair was tied back in a loose ponytail with a silk sunflower clipped above her left ear. "I have no idea what I did to deserve that man."

"You're kind, fun, beautiful," I piped in, "and he's just treating you exactly how you deserve to be treated. Happy Birthday, love."

"Nattie!" Laura squealed. "I can't wait for tonight. It's been ages since we all went out together."

"That's because I'm a big buzzkill and my stupid body won't let me get wasted with you."

"You don't have to drink to go out with us," she pulled me in for a long uncomfortable hug. "You're still you and we love you."

"I know," I forced a smile.

Admitting it to myself made me feel like a horrible person, but I didn't enjoy being sober while they were drinking. They tended to get rude and obnoxious without realizing it and my sober brain wasn't equipped to brush things off as easily as I could when I had a good buzz going. But, to say that it felt like a chore to be their sober third wheel was an understatement. But it's just the way things had to be.

On one occasion, I bought a bottle of wine, thinking I could pass out and sleep deeply enough to escape the nightmares. The moment I took the tiniest sip, I started throwing up so violently I could hardly take a breath between heaves. I tried to call Laura, but I couldn't even speak to tell her what was happening. Luckily, she drove straight over, climbed in through my kitchen window and found me on my living room floor. She got me out to the car and to the hospital where they ran every test imaginable but found nothing wrong. I soon discovered that any kind of alcohol I tried to drink resulted in the same violent rebellion of my body. As my health issues intensified, I realized it wasn't just the wine - I had developed an intolerance for anything fried or processed too.

At first, doctors were concerned that it was some sort of allergy, but they were never able to pin down exactly what the cause was. Through trial and error, all I had come to know for sure was that I had to keep my diet perfectly clean at all times if I didn't want to spend the next 24 hours dry heaving and possibly end up in the ER again. Abiola and Laura were always supportive through all of it, accompanying me to doctor visits, always making sure to check on me, driving me to the hospital when I couldn't get there myself. I couldn't have asked for better people to have in my corner. However, now that I was on a strict diet, the road to recovery was pretty lonely. I knew I had become significantly less fun to hang out with.

The girls would always tease me about how put together my life was. Sure, it looked good on paper; top-rated artist in my department, an amazing house which I always kept immaculate, and when I wasn't working, I was at the gym. They seemed to think that I had a perfect life. They had no idea how much I envied them. They both had incredible relationships with gorgeous men who doted on them endlessly. They were always commenting on how jealous they were of my body, but they also never missed a chance to eat delicious foods that I couldn't so much as smell without getting sick. They didn't realize that my house was always clean because it was empty and sterile; just like the rest of my life.

I didn't even have a pet. Ever since little Ivan died, I accepted that I wasn't pet owner material. If I couldn't keep a goldfish alive, what chance did I have with a more complex and emotionally dependent animal? Besides, with my work schedule, it would be cruel to even try.

"Before we get started with what we've got on today, I need to ask you guys a really important favor," Abiola said, circling the desk to take both mine and Laura's hands in hers. "The two of you have been such a huge part of my life. You've been there for me through all my family drama and I couldn't love you more if you were my flesh and blood sisters."

"Abi," Laura pushed out her bottom lip. "That's the sweetest thing you could possibly say."

"Well, I would be so honored if the two of you would be my bridesmaids this spring. Please say yes!"

The three of us all wrapped our arms around each other in a sickeningly sweet display of female solidarity. I forced a smile and swallowed the lump in my throat as I imagined walking down the aisle on the arm of some random groomsman who had a wife or girlfriend somewhere in the church. This would be the second time I was a bridesmaid at someone's wedding. The old saying 'three times a bridesmaid, never a bride' rang out in my mind.

"I would love to be a bridesmaid at your wedding," Laura crooned.

I mustered the minimal amount of excitement I could get away with for the situation and said, "Me too. I love you, woman," then patted Abiola on the back.

Abiola nodded and wiped at eyeliner from beneath her watering eyes. She was an old soul with a soft heart. She spent her weekends volunteering at a children's group home. That was where she met her fiancé Trevor, and they bonded over their dysfunctional family situations. They would probably adopt a bunch of foster kids right after their wedding and live happily ever after. She deserved that; it was all she ever wanted.

"Okay ladies," Abiola clapped her hands. "Today we're looking for something we can use for the promotion of the OSA campus, which will be opening next year in Portland, Oregon. Boss says our primary focus is to attract engineering and architectural students for the Lunar retreat that's in the works."

"So, where do we start?" Laura said, looking right at me.

"I am going to need to work up some concept drawings for the Lunar Resort. Also, if you could give me the clearest photos of the most beautiful views the Lunar Surface has to offer, that would be cool to show exactly what the students should be aspiring to be a part of. I want to see some dramatic landscapes with visible craters, maybe some rock formations. Anything to pull people in."

"I'm on it," Laura nodded and sat down at her touch responsive computer.

"I'll go to engineering to get permission to use blueprints of the resort that you can use to make the concept drawings," Abiola said, then turned and headed towards the elevator.

It was an exciting project. I used to fantasize that by the time I was ready to retire, I would be able to cash in on all the vacation time I had accrued and maybe even spend a few of my golden years at that resort. The thought of waking up in the morning and looking out the window to see the Earth just as we see the moon from down here always gave me a sense of calm.

Four hours later, all final decisions had been made on what I wanted to use on the project. Right on cue, my trusty assistants started complaining that they were starving to death.

"If I don't get some corned beef nachos in me in the next ten minutes, I might actually die," Laura said and stood up dramatically from her desk.

"I want waffles and bacon," Abiola rubbed her belly.

I sighed at the memory of bacon; I would probably just have some raw vegetables and berries. I was still looking at my screen and inspecting one of the photos, trying to decide on how I would alter the image to bring it to life. My eyes burned. I clenched them shut and rubbed them, forcing them to rest. Eye strain was the enemy and this day was proving to be particularly difficult since I had hardly slept the night before. I couldn't shake my anxiety about today's social gathering after work. Stress and lack of sleep usually meant a big fat migraine, which was the last thing I needed at Laura's party.

"I'm going to head to the chill room. I need a nap more than anything."

"You better be rested for tonight's festivities," Laura wagged her finger at me.

"I'll bring my party face, I promise," I said. I stood up but couldn't stop the oncoming yawn. "The fatigue is killing me."

"Yeah, no coffee or sugar in your morning will do that to you," Abiola said with a shake of her head. "I don't know how you do it."

"Well, it's easy since a cup of coffee could put me in the hospital again, I guess."

"Jesus," Abiola pressed her fist to her mouth. "I didn't mean to…"

"It's fine, Abi," I assured her. "I just need to get a little rest."

The two girls headed down to the food court while I made my way to the sleeping pods. White, plush, and stacked like a honeycomb, they were an inviting image that screamed comfort. I smiled and breathed a sigh of relief to find my favorite lower level pod was unoccupied. Turning on the sound system, I selected a playlist I knew I could sleep through. Sometimes I would choose guided meditation tracks or audiobooks. Today's selection was soft cello. Something about the deep tones helped me unwind no matter what was on my mind. I settled in, turning on the heated cushions and closing my eyes.

I practiced the deep breathing exercises the doctor had taught me as I pictured myself floating through a dark endless sky toward the moon's surface. The pictures I had looked at for over four hours served to be the subject of my meditation. I inhaled deeply, focusing on relaxing my arms and legs. Exhaling, I imagined moving further out into space. In… and out…

As soon as sleep found me, I was swept up in a flurry of blinding light. My stomach turned as the light began strobing violently, causing me to feel disoriented. My body tensed as I realized it had been several weeks since I'd had an episode. Right on schedule, it hit me like a ton of bricks.

*Oh no, no, no, no... I can't deal with this right now, not at work!*

I struggled to wake myself, I couldn't move. The cold sensation of a smooth metallic surface beneath me was confusing. I felt my fingertips twitch as I tried desperately to flail any and all limbs that might respond to my will, but my body remained where it was. I strained to sit up or scream, but I couldn't even open my mouth. I was trapped, overwhelmed by the weight of my chest collapsing in on itself. If I didn't put every ounce of will I possessed into sucking air through my nostrils, I had a very real fear that my body would simply shut down, leaving my body as a cold stiff corpse which might be found hours later in my cozy little pod. Filling my lungs with intention, I gasped for air, breath after panicked breath, hoping someone would notice and wake me.

The strobing intensified for what felt like several minutes and when it finally stopped, there remained a constant blinding light that made my eyes water. Tears streamed from the outer corners of my eyes into my ears.

"Help... me..." I managed to whisper to no one in particular.

From the edge of my vision, a blurry figure leaned over me.

"Please," I sobbed, trying to turn my head to get a better look at who it was, but I couldn't.

My chest burned as my heart pounded out of control. I tried to calm myself by reciting the scientific facts about what I knew was happening.

*During REM sleep, your muscles are essentially turned off to keep you from sleepwalking. When a person wakes up during REM, they are fully conscious but completely paralyzed. Usually, physical stimulation from someone rubbing or shaking them will pull the victim out of the purgatorial state. Unfortunately, living alone means I have no one to rescue me during these episodes, which can sometimes last for hours.*

"Just close your eyes. Everything will be okay," a distorted voice spoke through the fog of my half-conscious state.

*Maybe my brain is morphing the cello music into a voice. Sleep paralysis is often accompanied by waking dreams or hallucinations, after all.*

I thought I could force myself to come out of it but, instead, I moved even deeper into unconsciousness. It wasn't like falling, but more like being underwater and sinking slowly. I struggled against what felt like a chemically induced calm. I tried again to force myself awake but couldn't. The darkness swallowed me up and I finally surrendered to it.

To my surprise, I suddenly found myself vividly aware of two things; one, the fact that I was breathing without much effort, and two, I was no longer in my cushioned sleeping pod, but rather stretched out flat on my back on a cold metal surface. All efforts to move just made me realize that what I was experiencing was very different from the sleep paralysis I was familiar with. I could move my fingers and flex my wrists and feet. There were actual *physical* restraints fastened around my wrists, neck, forehead, and ankles that were preventing me from moving.

Blinking hard, I strained to look around at my surroundings. The entire room was reflective as if every surface and object was made from surgical steel. It was shockingly cold, almost like the inside of a walk-in refrigerator. I grunted, twisting my wrists in hopes that I could slip out the straps.

There was a continuous hum that was so low I didn't hear it so much as felt it vibrating through my entire body. There was a spherical light that seemed to be floating in the air a few feet over me. The ceiling was high above that and almost too dark for me to make out anything but the vague shape of what might have been a reflection of myself and the rest of the room around me. I strained to see past the light so I could study what else I could make out in the reflective ceiling. My heart pounded in my ears as my attention was drawn to a distorted human shape in the darkness at my side.

A chill spread through my body as I realized that someone, or something, was quietly watching me struggle but I couldn't for the life of me work out who, as the silhouette disappeared from my view the moment I noticed it. Even when I turned my eyes as far as I could, the dark corners of the room remained completely obscured. Regardless of the deafening silence and the fact that I couldn't see anyone, I knew someone was there.

# Chapter
## TWO

"Who's there?" I demanded loudly, though my trembling voice gave away my fear.

Off to my left, a dark shape moved towards me. They were by my side before I knew it and I let out a small scream as a hand clapped over my mouth and nose.

"Make another sound and we are both dead. Do you understand?" A deep voice said in a hushed tone.

I looked up to find a face looking down at me. He had angular features and blue-tinted skin now clearly visible, and the sensation of his hand smothering my scream was unmistakably real. This was no hallucination attributed to my sleep disorder.

"I need you to be very quiet," he whispered in the same deep smooth voice. "For *both* our sakes," he added.

I gathered my wits, blinking once deliberately as if to nod in agreement, and slowed my breathing to demonstrate I had calmed down. He removed his hand and nodded.

"Good," he said. He stood taller and smoothed down his grey uniform. "I do not want to have to put you under again."

"Who are you?" I asked, making sure that my voice was no louder than his.

Blinking hard again, I tried to focus on his face. If I made it out of this alive, the police would need a description of this psycho. I could feel him touching my arm, but I couldn't see what he was doing.

"I'm Korin."

I studied the details of his face and noticed that his cheekbones and jawline were extremely angular. In fact, all his features were.

"Could you elaborate a bit, Korin?" I said, trying to keep him engaged with some conversation, but a lingering thought kept chilling me to the core, making it hard to imagine having a real chat with this man. I couldn't help but wonder if he planned on letting me live since he was so comfortable letting me see his face.

He raised an eyebrow, then said, "I am your doctor."

As soon as he said it, my attempt at keeping cool became doubly difficult. There was no way I wanted to play doctor with this freak. I noted there must have been a blue light somewhere in the vicinity casting an iridescent glow over him.

"No, my doctor is a short Asian woman named Alicia Wang," I asserted. "You don't look like a short Asian woman to me."

"No, I'm not human and we are not on Earth."

"Oh my god, you're out of your mind," I said louder than I meant to.

"Keep your voice quiet."

"HEL…" He clapped his hand over my mouth and nose again.

"We are aboard a large medical vessel orbiting your planet, the E-Orbiter-3," he said then leaned over me and looked intensely into my eyes. "How else do you explain your presence here?"

"Ow," I groaned as he took his hand away to let me speak. "You drugged me and…"

"And walked into a building riddled with high definition security cameras, and armed guards where I carried an unconscious woman out of the door without being stopped by anyone?"

"I… I don't know," I whined. "I can't think. I can't move. I'm freaking the fuck out!" I shouted and started to cry.

"If I remove the straps across your forehead and neck, will you calm down and cooperate?"

"Yes," I managed to say in between the sobs that were shaking my body.

I looked up at him, my eyes clouding with tears. He sighed, looking into my eyes before shaking his head and unfastening the straps, as though he knew it was a bad idea but was doing it anyway.

Finally, free to move my head, I looked down in horror at my body. My clothes had been rolled up and he had various intravenous tubes inserted all along my arms, legs, and abdomen.

"Holy shit! What are you doing to me?" I shrieked.

"I need you to keep your voice down. I am trying to help you," he said as he fiddled with one of the tubes that was in my left arm. I also noticed that there was not a blue light cast over my body. Seeing his hand grasp my arm, I could see that his skin had a real blue tint to it.

I winced as he pulled the needle out.

"Why is this happening to me?" I said.

A bloody hole about the diameter of a pencil marked the spot where he had pulled the needle out.

"I'm here to help you."

"Please, just let me go," I pleaded. "If you want money, I can get you money."

He took a small device that was the size of a little flashlight and pressed it onto the needle hole. To my astonishment, when he removed it, my wound was completely healed.

"Natalia," he said quietly moving to the next tube and repeating the process. "I do not want anything from you."

"How do you know my name?"

"You are on an alien spacecraft and you're asking how I know your name?"

"You don't have to be an asshole."

He clenched his jaw and he took a breath as if to gather his patience.

"You need to take me back home, right now," I ordered.

"You can either cooperate or go back to being paralyzed," he said calmly in a way that told me that he meant it.

I realized that I could finally focus on his eyes, which were a stunning mixture of violet and purple with silver flecks that reminded me of the Keystone Asterism in the Hercules constellation. Clouds of gasses in space left over from the birth of a star created colors that most people never got the chance to see in a natural setting. I certainly didn't expect to see those colors contained in the eyes of a man.

As he pulled out the final needle from my abdomen, I felt my muscles cramp and tighten around the metal.

"I have to do one more procedure before I can send you home. I know you often get cravings for things you used to eat before, but I need you to promise you will not try to eat or drink the things that have made you sick in the past. No prescription medication, no processed foods, no alcohol. If you do, you could very possibly die. Do you understand?"

I didn't answer but nodded in agreement.

"Good. This may cause you some discomfort. I need you to keep your palm flat and open for me," he instructed.

He took a small blade from a tray and sat down on the right side of the table and ran his fingertips over the palm of my hand. I imagined him slitting my wrist and letting me quietly bleed out in whatever weird storage room we were in. Against my better judgment, I uncurled my fingers, offering him my open palm. There was a sharp sting as he made the small incision. He then used something that looked like long tweezers to pick up a tiny metallic pebble and dipped it in a flesh-colored liquid which appeared to be some kind of fast drying silicone, he placed it inside the open incision and used the healing device to seal the wound.

Once again, the fresh wound disappeared right in front of my eyes, while my brain struggled to understand how anything like this was possible. Everything else, this place, all the freaky medical equipment, his oddly alien appearance, could all be explained away. It could be one elaborate prank that someone who didn't know me well had decided to pull. It was a far-fetched explanation, but an explanation nonetheless. But watching my flesh be opened up and closed before my eyes without even a scar left behind defied all logic.

"What did you just put into my body?"

"Something to help you return."

"No offense, Korin, but I think I'd rather just live with whatever you're trying to cure."

"I need to see you back here in 15 hours. This is non-negotiable," he said, picking up a metallic object. It was reflective, just like everything else in the room, but it was irregular in shape; not perfectly round but smooth and about the size of a peach pit. "When the time comes, hold this and focus on your memory of this place."

"Sure," I said sarcastically.

He didn't acknowledge my obvious unwillingness to return but simply stuck a needle in my arm, plunging me towards unconsciousness once again.

"You can't force medical…" I slowly moved my head back and forth and babbled incoherently, "treatment on…"

But I wasn't able to finish my statement as I found myself traveling through space once more. The strobing light was almost hypnotic, and I felt my entire body go limp. I wasn't fully aware of my arms or legs in the sense that I would normally feel my extremities. Rather, I was aware that I existed, and of my surroundings and all the splendid lights in the vast sea of darkness that was washing me onward through space.

## CHAPTER TWO

When I woke, it was with a deep and sudden gasp, as I sat straight up in my pod. My heart was pounding through my ribcage as I reached for my phone, noticing a metallic object that fell out of my hand.

"What... the... actual... fuck?"

# Chapter
## THREE

I picked up the shiny stone and looked at it. Maybe it fell out of someone's pocket into my hand when they were napping in the pod above my own? I stuck it into my purse so that I could take a closer look at it later and looked at the time displayed on my phone.

"Shit!" I jumped up to rush back to my desk. An hour had passed, and I was sure that my assistants were wondering where I had gone.

Laura and Abiola both looked up as I approached.

"Good morning, sunshine!" Laura crooned.

"I was starting to think you'd been abducted," Abiola said with a raised eyebrow.

"I guess I was even more tired than I realized," I responded sheepishly.

I rubbed my face. It had all felt so real. The lights and machines that were all around me, the feeling of the needles, and that strange man all seemed as clear and real as the desk I was leaning on.

"You're going to make it tonight, right?" Laura frowned. I had a bad habit of canceling when it came to socializing after work.

"Of course," I smiled and reached across my desk to put my shaky hand on hers. "I wouldn't miss it."

The three of us got back to work, Laura and Abiola on the tasks I had assigned to them earlier and I started on the digital sketches for the concept art for the Lunar Resort. As I moved my wrist, the stylus glided over the smooth touch-screen. I tried to immerse myself in the beautiful world of lines and colors. I didn't want to think about the nightmare. That man's face seemed so familiar. I bit my lip as I pondered why that was the case. Maybe it was a dream based on someone I had seen in passing at the gym or somewhere else in the OSA building. As silly as it felt, I found myself fixated on a childish idea that I could find him.

The workday flew by much faster than I would have liked, and the moment I had been dreading arrived – it was time for the celebrations to begin. I wanted to tell Laura and Abiola about the dream. I couldn't stop thinking about it and I was worried that whatever was going on might be alluding to my sleep disorder getting worse. I decided against it. Today was supposed to be about Laura. The last thing I wanted was to take over her birthday with my depressing bullshit.

"Woo! Let's head out, ladies," Laura said, standing up and stretching her arms over her head. "I'm starving for some onion rings."

"Forget your onion rings," Abiola said. She picked up her purse "I want a Long Island."

I pressed my lips together, trying to think about what I was looking forward to, but I had absolutely nothing positive to contribute so I tried the first thing that popped into my head.

"It'll be nice to get out of the house," I lied, attempting to convince myself that it wasn't going to be as bad as I expected.

"Have a nice night, ladies. Thank you for all your hard work," the A.I. said as we made our way through the lobby.

"Thank you. Goodnight," I responded.

"You're so weird," Laura said, hooking her arm through mine.

We exited the building and walked to *The Cube*, which was Laura's favorite club, located only a few blocks away from the OSA. It was accented with neon green lights and was sleek and modern. It played decent music and served strong drinks. I understood the appeal – I would have loved it myself were it not for the fact that I couldn't eat or drink anything available there except bottled water.

As soon as we walked in, the hostess took our jackets and purses so we could dance without worrying about losing our stuff. Our tabs would be paid through transfers via our smart-bands. Wallets filled with cards, money and identification had become mostly obsolete by the year 2025 as most working professionals used smart bracelets that held all their personal and banking information. Each bracelet was programmed to activate only when worn by the person who owned them. A small sensor on the inner rim of the bracelet was able to read DNA codes through contact with the wearer's skin. Now that I'd had it for such a long time, it seemed unthinkable that society functioned without them once.

The three of us went straight to the bar where a handsome blonde bartender, probably in his early 20s, greeted us with a smile.

"What can I get for you lovely ladies?" he asked, his grin widening in that professional way that only servers could pull off without seeming like they were leering at you.

"We'd like two shots of tequila followed by a blended mango margarita and a long island iced tea," Laura announced.

The bartender poured two shots and slid them over to Laura and Abiola.

"What about your pretty friend?" He gestured to me and my cheeks got hot.

"I'll just have bottled water, please."

"Designated driver?"

"No," Laura downed her shot and smacked her lips together a couple of times. "She's just allergic to fun."

"I'm medically incapable of drinking alcohol," I said and swatted Laura on the arm. "It's not by choice. Believe me."

"You're right," Laura backpedaled as if realizing how catty she had sounded.

The bartender's welcoming expression had been replaced by one of discomfort. He handed over my bottle of water. I knew Laura didn't mean anything by it, but it was still embarrassing. Fortunately, the feeling didn't linger for too long. The three of us headed to the dancefloor and danced for a few songs, only returning to the bar when the girls wanted more shots.

Seeing that my water bottle was empty, Laura pulled me back to the bar and waved to get the bartender's attention, calling out, "Can we get another water over here, sir?"

"Sure thing," he smiled, showing a prominent dimple in his right cheek.

"You know, she's actually really fun," Laura slurred her words as she tried to repair the awkwardness from earlier. "Natalia is awesome… if you eat really, really clean and love working out… which it looks like you do," she continued, then reached forward to clumsily squeeze his bicep. "I'm going to run to the lady's room. Wait here," she ordered me.

As soon as she was out of earshot the bartender leaned on his elbows and whispered under the music, "Is she always such a bitch?"

My eyes snapped forward and locked with his and it took every ounce of self-control at my disposal not to grab the nearest cocktail and splash it right in his smug face.

"Yeah," I stood up straight. "She was a real bitch when she used to spend hours holding my hair back while I puked my guts out at work. She was even bitchier when she would sit with me in the ER lobby holding my hand, waiting for me to get seen when she could have been at home, in bed with her man."

"I'm sorry, I didn't mean…"

"Forget it," I cut him off and took the bottled water as I headed off to the bathroom to find Laura.

She probably only asked me to wait there because she wanted to give me a chance to flirt with that asshole. So much for that. Laura's boyfriend Alex had intercepted her on her way back from the restroom. In one hand he balanced a small but ornate birthday cake, complete with candles. His other hand was busy running its fingers through Laura's hair as he pulled her in for a passionate kiss. Watching them together made me painfully aware of the void in my life.

It had been years since a man had touched me that way. I had been on all the popular dating apps through college. I even hooked up several times, but I always felt disappointed and grossed out afterward.

Soon, Abiola's fiancé Trevor joined the party and we all gathered around a table and waited for the bartender to show up with some matches to light the candles. I had always hated birthdays. My father wasn't around much when I was young. He called and talked to me on the phone a couple of times a year. In spite of my making straight A's in school and doing everything I could to make him proud, he rarely showed his face. I remember when he promised that he would come to see me blow out the candles on my tenth birthday cake. I believed him. No matter how many times my mother would tell me not to get my hopes up, I was sure that he would be there.

Mom had procrastinated bringing the cake out for as long as she could. But then time ran out and I was left sat at the table staring down at those candles like they were my hopes and dreams going up in flames, I couldn't bring myself to blow them out. Mom ended up doing the honors for me. I held it together and after the cake was served, I thanked everyone for coming. Then, I went up to my room where I sobbed quietly until every last guest had gone home. An hour or so later, there was a knock at the door. I leaped off my bed and ran downstairs, hoping beyond all hope that my birthday would have a happy ending after all.

Of course, it wasn't my father at the door; just a delivery man holding a brightly wrapped package with a bright blue bow on it. I remember how my hands trembled as I carefully pulled off the wrapping paper. It was a telescope and a note from my father apologizing for not being able to make it. I didn't take the parts out of the box for almost a month. But the first time I looked through the lens, the sight of the astral bodies so far beyond the world I knew took my breath away. I was filled with wonder and couldn't stop looking up that night and wondering about the mysteries that lay above me.

Thus began my love affair with the stars. My paintings allowed me to share the emotions I otherwise had a difficult time articulating. Every time I created a new piece, I couldn't help but secretly hope that my father would see it and feel what I felt while I painted it. If that were true, maybe in a roundabout way, we were still connected.

I snapped myself out of the memory and watched Laura blow out the candles.

"What did you wish for?" Alex asked, taking her into his arms.

"I actually forgot to make a wish," she smiled. "I guess I already have everything I want."

I swallowed my heartache and mustered a smile for my beautiful friend, hating myself for feeling anything but joy to hear her say something like this.

"Happy Birthday, Laura," I said. I pulled her into an embrace and kissed her cheek. "I've got to head out. I'm still not feeling so hot."

"Oh, I understand, honey," she said, but clung to me a little longer. "Thank you so much for coming out with us. I know it's hard, but it meant so much to have you here. I miss hanging out with you outside of work."

"Yeah, me too."

I buried my pain. Even though Laura hadn't meant anything by it when she commented on me being allergic to fun, it hurt; mostly because it was essentially true. There wasn't any room in my life for the little poisons that made life more palatable. Who in their right mind would want to share my perfectly sterile life?

I pretended that the only thing I cared about was my artwork and my job. But deep down, the thing I wanted most out of life was to feel loved and accepted for who I really was. I wanted someone who found joy, just in being around me, even with my issues. I would have liked to have blamed the lack of romance in my life on my health problems alone, but the truth was much harder to admit. I was a horrible judge of character and I didn't trust myself to let the right person into my life.

I conceded that it was better to just accept my life as it was and be grateful for everything I did have. My thoughts returned to the man from my dream; Korin.

He was pretty convincing as a doctor. But in all my trips to the hospital and my own physician, I had never seen anyone who even remotely resembled him. I was certain that, if I had, I would have remembered, no matter what shape I was in at the time.

I reached the gated community where my grand modern home was located and trudged up the walkway to the front door. As soon as my smart-band registered in the lock, I felt a wave of relief wash over me. Finally safe and sound from any uncomfortable social interactions, for the night at least, I could unwind the only way I knew how. After having a modest dinner, I cleaned my already immaculate kitchen and ran myself a bath complete with sweet-smelling natural oils in the water and lit scented candles on the edge of the tub.

When I got out, I set to work laying out my outfit for the next morning. A sensible black pencil skirt and a pressed white button-up seemed appropriate for a Tuesday. Placing my purse on the dresser, I thought again about the metal stone. Curiously, I slowly slipped my hand into my purse and felt around for it, half hoping it would be gone and that I had only imagined finding it in my hand when I woke up. To my dismay, I felt the cool smooth object. I took it out to look at it more closely. I turned on my lamp and turned it over in my hand. It didn't look like anything high tech, more like one of those shiny stones you see in bamboo planters, but larger.

I moved my thumb in a circle over the reflective surface, triggering a flurry of images to flash through my mind, of Korin's face and all those tubes hanging out of my body.

Fifteen hours… I looked at my phone wondering what time it was when he said that.

*It doesn't matter.* I shook my head. *This little thing doesn't mean anything.*

I clenched my fist around the shiny little bastard and marched straight into the kitchen where I threw it unceremoniously into the trash and went on with my nightly routine. I exfoliated, brushed my teeth, blow dried my hair, and put on my favorite pajamas. When I was finally tucked into bed, I took a deep breath.

It was a bad episode, I told myself. The worst one yet… but that meant that it would be several weeks before I had to deal with another one. My sleep disorder worked in cycles. I might not be able to control it, but at least I was learning to live with it. If I knew what to expect, I could stop living in fear of my disease and live my best life, regardless. At least there would be no scary blue guy sticking needles in my body. Everything was going to be okay.

I turned on my sound system and put on a guided meditation, feeling newly empowered by my level-headedness. I drifted off and slept the deepest most peaceful dreamless sleep that I had since I could remember.

At the first glimpse of dawn, I opened my eyes and took a deep and calming breath. The sun was filtering in through my windows, casting a warm glow over the entire room. When my feet touched the soft beige carpet, I stood and stretched, noting the absence of the fog that usually shrouded my consciousness for the first hour after dragging myself out of bed. I looked at the vintage analog clock hanging next to my doorway, which read 6:00 AM.

That can't be right. I looked down at my phone which sat on my nightstand. It lit up as it recognized my face and displayed the time. 6:01 AM. *Huh?* My alarm wasn't going to go off for another hour. Nice.

# Chapter
## FOUR

I took a moment to re-evaluate how I was feeling. I wasn't anxious or under-rested. I didn't feel the need to go back to bed. In fact, I couldn't wait to get my day started. I walked to my window to see my neighborhood bathed in the early morning light that I had long forgotten. Walking to my kitchen, I started thinking of all the things I might do with my stolen hour.

Breakfast was simple now that I couldn't eat anything processed; sweet berries and crunchy almonds washed down with a tall glass of chilled lemon-water. I pulled my yoga mat off the closet shelf and spent 30 minutes repeating a series of simple asanas to clear my mind and loosen up my muscles. I turned on a playlist from a series of astronomy podcasts I had fallen behind on. I listened intently as I took my time putting on my makeup.

As I started blending my foundation, I noticed there was an odd light shining across my face. Looking all around, I tried to find the source. It wasn't constant, but rather slowly intensified and just as slowly faded out. Dread began to build up in me as I thought about the lights I normally saw when I was experiencing sleep paralysis. Was I asleep right now and only dreaming that I had woken up early? Or was I having some sort of seizure?

As soon as the thought passed I glimpsed at my wrist and saw a strange light that was shining through my skin. As it faded, I looked in the mirror and held my arm out to the side. The veins throughout the length of my arm slowly lit up again as if the blood in my arm was pulsating and exuding a brilliant bluish-white light.

*I don't have time for this.* My panicked thoughts gave way to denial. *I'm probably hallucinating anyway.* I put a cardigan on to cover my arms and threw on some mascara before rushing out the door. There was no way I was going to run late after waking up an hour early. I needed to make an appointment with my doctor and get on some anti-psychotics. People with mental illness find ways to cope and function every single day. This was nothing to worry about, I told myself.

I walked at my usual pace and tried my absolute best to pretend like this was just like every other morning. *Everything is fine. Today is a regular day. I will get to work, start the next task and smash it like I always do.* But as I passed the first few people on the sidewalk, their wide eyes and furrowed brows told me that something was wrong. Losing my grip on what little semblance of calm I was still clinging to, I turned around and ran all the way back home.

By the time I reached my bathroom mirror, the lights were now shining in bright glowing veins through my forehead, temples, and cheeks as well as each side of my neck. I stripped down to my underwear to find my fears were confirmed. Every major vein in my body was glowing through my skin.

"Shit!"

I threw my clothes on, rushed to my kitchen, flung the lid off the trash can, and started digging through the garbage like a lunatic. As soon as I spotted the silver stone, I snatched it up and ran to my bedroom. Closing my eyes and attempting to slow my breathing, I tried to remember what he said. What was it? Something about focusing on the memory of that location?

*Focus, Natalia.* I clenched my fist around the stone and held it to my chest and soon felt myself floating. I was acutely aware of what happened next. I sensed I was moving upward, the pressure intensifying as if I were traveling in a fast elevator, but there wasn't any discomfort; just the knowledge that I was moving upward. I could see the roof of my house becoming smaller and smaller before disappearing into a spectacular view of my block, Las Vegas, then the edge of the Pacific Ocean. Glancing to my right, I could see the thin blue line that was our atmosphere, separating Earth's surface from the darkness of space.

My vision was then obscured by the same bright light that had so often haunted my dreams. But in a matter of seconds, it faded, and I found my bare feet planted firmly on a cold metal surface. Hesitantly, I turned around to see a soft light illuminating a chrome metal table that seemed to levitate in the center of the otherwise dark room.

Beyond the table, I saw a sinister-looking machine equipped with the familiar needles and tubes from my last visit. My heart beating in my ears was the only sound in the seemingly vacant room and my anxiety was growing every passing moment. It wasn't until the sight of a window stole my attention that I really started to calm down. I approached slowly, still uncertain of what had just taken place and feeling unsteady on my feet. The window was small, no bigger than a porthole on a submarine. I wouldn't have even seen the window at all had it not been for the bluish planet that caught my eye. It hung suspended in the vast cavern of the universe, perfect and solitary as if it was waiting for me to notice it.

My breath was stolen as I blinked away tears at the vision before me. All my life, I had longed for this view of Earth. Knowing I would never be an astronaut, the best chance I had ever had of seeing this was by working my ass off for OSA long enough to earn a ticket to the Lunar Resort.

"Wow," I said out loud.

Just then a door slid open and I jumped, looking around in vain for a place to hide. Korin stepped through the door and it automatically closed behind him. I relaxed and turned once more to look out the window.

"You are late," he said with narrowed eyes. "I had to step away for a moment. I have a constricting schedule today."

"You're sorry? I'm freaking glowing!" I said holding my arms out.

"I did tell you that you had to be back here in 15 hours. You should have followed my instructions," he retorted unsympathetically.

"Honestly, I thought that the whole thing was a nightmare."

"Under the circumstances, I would think you would be grateful for my assistance."

"Oh really, and why is that?"

"Because the nanobots have removed all tracking and monitoring technology from your body."

"Nanobots?" My eyes widened.

"Yes. However, if I leave them in much longer, they will attack your immune system and organs."

"What?" I shrieked, "You put tiny robots in my body, without my consent I might add. And now, you're saying that if I hadn't made it back in time, they would have started eating my organs?"

"Attacking your organs, actually, but it would amount to the same general result."

"How dare you act like this is no big deal!"

"Stop shouting. Unless you would prefer to have the monitorial devices replaced."

"This is impossible. I shouldn't be here," I started to whimper, and his face suddenly looked a little distressed.

"I had little time for a proper explanation when I saw you last. I told you I was here to help you and that you should listen to me."

"How do I know you're here to help me? How do I know that you're not just experimenting on me?"

"The only data you have to go on is my word, I'm afraid. Shall we extract the nanobots, or would you prefer I send you back?"

"Fine," I said. I wiped the tears from my eyes and walked towards him. "Yes, get them out. I have to get back and get to work. My coworkers are expecting me, and I have a job to do."

"Your job is of little consequence to me," he motioned toward the metallic table.

"That's because you're an asshole," I said hopping up on the table and laying down.

"I fail to see how my opinion of your pointless employment makes me…" he paused as if trying to find an alternate word but then gave in and said, "an asshole."

"Because my job is important to me," I said. "I've worked really hard for a good portion of my life to advance to the position I hold right now."

"Does this bring you gratification?" he asked, cleaning off the crease in my elbow where he was about to insert a needle.

"It's the highest I can go and still do artwork. Anything above me and I would have to work in administration and management of other artists so, my job is exactly where I want to be."

He inserted a needle, making me wince as it sliced into my skin effortlessly, but I was relieved to find that the pain vanished as quickly as it appeared. It had a long tube attached to it and ran to the machine. He touched the machine which started pulsating at the same frequency as the light shining through my skin. The luminous material slowly started moving out of my body through the tube and returning to the machine.

I had always been open to the idea of extraterrestrial life existing somewhere in the infinite universe. Science has long accepted the possibility that we are not alone. However, the last thing I expected was to see it proven in my lifetime; let alone find myself face to face with a humanoid creature from another world. My intense resistance to believing that this was actually happening was overruled by what my senses were telling me. The sights, sounds, and smells were all far too visceral to be a dream, and in spite of how ridiculous the situation may have appeared, I could almost feel my psyche shifting to accept what was clearly undeniable.

"It's good that you are happy in your current profession. Depression and anxiety caused by unfavorable working conditions can limit an individual's productivity. Although…" he hesitated.

"What?" I raised an eyebrow.

"I fail to understand the human fascination with art. Your primitive satellites capture reasonably accurate images."

"When I render my interpretation of those images," I sighed, searching for words that could make him understand, "I intensify the colors or make subtle adjustments to provoke emotions from people."

"You are giving them a false sense of the universe by changing what is into what you want it to be," he said while looking at a screen that was displaying line after line of alien text across it.

"It's not about misrepresenting what the universe looks like. I want people to share the wonderment I feel when I look at those images. I might exaggerate them, but if they saw the original images," I struggled to find my point, "most people wouldn't appreciate the true scale of it all. I offer them a chance to feel what I feel when I look at the stars."

"So, art is not about accurate imagery, it's about conveying the emotions of the artist?" He looked at me quizzically.

"Sometimes," I said with a shrug.

He looked back at his screen.

"Humans are strange creatures - they crave emotions just as they struggle to gain control of them."

"What do you mean?"

"More advanced races have moved past relying on emotions in favor of logic to determine right and wrong. Emotions are chemical reactions in the brain that can negatively impact proper judgment."

"If that's the case, then why are you even allowing me to stay conscious while you do all this? Why not just keep me sedated?"

"The anesthesia seemed to have an adverse effect on you, causing intense distress. Seeing you in that condition caused me discomfort and I felt that the best way for me to work efficiently was to limit distractions by alleviating your suffering."

"You mean you felt bad for me?" My brow furrowed.

"I suppose that isn't an inaccurate statement."

"That's called empathy. It's one of those pesky emotions you were just referring to."

"That just illustrates my point," he asserted. "If I had simply continued to administer the anesthesia, I would be paying full attention to what I'm doing rather than conversing with you. Thus, it was an error in judgment caused by the aforementioned emotion."

"Would you prefer me to be quiet?" I asked.

"I don't have a preference. I'm simply trying to read the reports collected by the nanobots."

I took a deep breath and looked down. The left side of my body had stopped glowing. They were making their way out. I relaxed, knowing that the ordeal was almost over.

"It appears that their prolonged presence in your system has caused a minimal amount of damage to your circulatory system."

"That's a good thing, right?" I looked at him and asked. "So, why do you sound worried?"

"The damage that was done needs to be repaired before I can send you back."

"Okay, well, how long will that take?"

"I can give you a healing accelerant, but I need to monitor your progress to ensure that it works properly and that you don't have an adverse reaction to it."

"So, are we talking a few minutes?"

"A few hours."

"Crap! Are you serious?"

He clenched his jaw before answering.

"I am serious."

I groaned and let my head fall back hard onto the metal surface.

"Would you prefer I administer the accelerant here and leave you alone, or would you like me to transfer you to my living quarters? You might find it more comfortable."

"Are you asking me if I want to go back to your place?"

Korin shifted his weight and pulled on the bottom of his shirt as if to straighten it, though it wasn't wrinkled to begin with.

"Yes," he said finally.

"I don't really want to sit in here for the next few hours. So, I guess I'll go with you."

I wasn't sure this was the best idea, but I figured, if he wanted to hurt me, he'd already had ample opportunity to do so.

"The corridors should be empty between here and my quarters," he reached out a hand to help me down from the table and I accepted it, if only as a gesture of trust.

"We must stay as quiet and discreet as possible. If anyone finds out that I'm allowing you to be here without the anesthesia…"

"Let me guess - you would be in big trouble?"

"We would both be in a great deal of trouble."

"I understand; quick and quiet," I nodded.

"But don't run."

"Okay."

After the last nanobots were out, Korin took a syringe and filled it with a clear liquid from a small bottle before placing a cap on the sharp end of the needle and putting it in his pocket. He opened a panel in the wall and retrieved a gray lab coat, which he offered me. I put it on, and we prepared to venture out into the corridor.

I walked close behind him, hoping that if someone were to glance in his direction, they wouldn't see me. The corridor was curved, dark, and featureless. The seamless walls were only broken by an occasional door. As we made a turn into a new wing I almost choked on my breath. It was bright white, and it was lined with several deep black doors, which seemed like gateways into endless nothingness. The floors, which were also a blinding white, had ripples of dark blue light slowly creeping across the wide hallway. My eyebrows furrowed as I fought with cognitive dissonance. *Am I seriously on an alien spaceship?* We hardly stepped forward when Korin pulled me around a corner and into another dark corridor, which eventually led into a more comfortable looking area with dim and warm lighting. I recoiled as we rushed past a few animated indoor plants and reached his door without incident, at which point I heard him breathe a sigh of relief.

Inside, the room contained sparse minimalist furniture. There was no wall art or pictures of any kind decorating the walls, and overall there was very little color. Everything was in varying shades of beige, white, and metallic colors. It appeared that everything was functional and had a practical purpose. It reminded me of those model homes that don't really look lived in, where there is nothing out of place. Everything is almost overly tidy and has a bland and empty feel to it. Then I realized with a jolt that, except for the lack of artwork, it was much like my own house.

I sat down on what I assumed was the equivalent of a couch. It was made up of three cubic-like structures with thin cushions on top of each other. I was surprised to find that it was more comfortable than it looked. Korin walked over to the wall and slid a panel open to reveal a shelf with a light.

"Would you like something to drink?" He asked over his shoulder.

"Yes please," I said, mainly accepting to be polite, although, in truth, I was not overly keen on the idea of consuming anything in this unusual place.

He entered a selection of numbers or letters into a touchscreen and a transparent bubble slowly formed under the light and began growing until it was about the size of a fist. It hung in the air, just levitating, rotating, and fluctuating in shape as if it was a water balloon.

He reached out, taking the formless blob into his hand and bringing it to me where I sat observing quietly. He offered me the balloon, which I took into my hand. It felt like I was holding a sphere made of gelatin. He returned to the shelf and repeated the process, taking his own gelatinous sphere once it was ready. Pursing his lips, he sucked on it slowly, demonstrating how to drink from it. I copied him, finding that it was filled with the most refreshing water I had ever tasted. As I pulled it away from my lips, I noticed that the thin membrane containing the liquid re-sealed itself, preventing anything from spilling out.

"Are you hungry?" Korin inquired.

"I actually have a very sensitive stomach. I would hate to get sick and make a mess all over your clean floor. But I appreciate the gesture."

"I am aware of your dietary needs and restrictions. I can offer you nutritious sustenance that will not cause you to become ill."

"So, you know what's wrong with me?"

"Physically? Yes."

"What is it exactly?"

"You have a parasite."

"A what?" I asked incredulously, finding myself somehow embarrassed and even a little offended. "What kind of parasite?"

"One that has not been discovered by Earth's medical sciences as of yet."

"Are you serious?"

"Why is it that you keep asking if I am serious? Is it common for humans to engage in humor while discussing their medical conditions?"

"No," I rolled my eyes. "It's a figure of speech. Where exactly is this parasite in my body?"

"I would prefer not to go into any further specifics, seeing as you are limited in your understanding of medical science. It makes conversations like these incredibly stressful and frustrating for me. Suffice to say that you are receiving the best possible treatment and, as long as you cooperate, you are expected to make a full recovery."

I put a hand on my forehead and asked, "I'm sorry, is this stressful for you?"

"Moderately stressful, yes," he responded, not detecting the sarcasm in my tone.

"I feel like I'm pointing out the obvious by saying that, since I'm the one with the parasite, I have more of a right to be stressed out than you do right now."

"That is understandable, but I have already told you that your condition is being treated."

I shook my head and put my face in my hands.

"Would it make you feel more at ease to know that most humans live their whole lives hosting numerous parasites and are never even aware of it?"

"Are you seri…" I stopped myself, took a breath, then started again. "Is that true?"

"Yes. In fact, undetected parasites are the root cause of many of your so-called mysterious diseases."

"Such as?"

"Schizophrenia, agoraphobia, obsessive-compulsive disorder, some forms of psychosis…"

"Wait a second," I interrupted. "Are you saying that mental illnesses are caused by parasites?"

"Not in every case," he said with a tilt of his head. "Mental illness can be caused by a number of energetic dissonances. However, it is often parasite-related."

"I never would've guessed that," I responded. Then, knowing he wasn't going to give me any more information about my condition, I made a conscious decision to allow him to change the subject, by saying, "Maybe you should get started with whatever you need to do so I can go home."

"Of course," he said politely with a single nod, then quickly went over to another wall panel and retrieved what looked like a first aid kit.

"You don't look like the extraterrestrials described by people who claim to have been abducted," I said lightly, trying to make conversation as he sat next to me and cleaned off the spot on my arm that he had chosen as the injection site.

He cracked a small bemused smile.

"The anesthesia acts as a memory suppressant. When the human brain retains a partial memory, it fills in the rest with whatever makes the most sense to them."

"So, there are no gray aliens?"

"Physically? Not that I am aware of."

"That's kind of comforting, I guess."

"Why is that?"

"Well, you don't look that different from us."

"I would have to disagree."

"Wow," I raised my eyebrows.

"I meant no offense, but you and I don't look anything alike."

"I mean other than the fact that your skin has a more interesting color."

"You think I look interesting?"

"Well, yes," I studied the details of his angular cheekbones and chiseled jaw. "Your features are so sharp compared to ours."

I tentatively touched his face and his expression softened. He seemed unsure of how to respond and simply pressed his lips together before bringing his focus back to the tasks at hand.

"I am going to inject you with the healing accelerant."

I nodded and turned my head away, clenching my eyes shut. I winced when I felt the mild sting.

"You have an aversion to receiving injections," he said.

"I don't like needles."

He softly took my earlobe between his thumb and forefinger to examine my pierced ears. The sensation of being touched in such a familiar way by a somewhat attractive man caught me off guard.

"It's different when you're getting a piercing," I blushed. "At the doctor's office, you're nervous and afraid. Knowing you'll get to wear beautiful earrings afterward makes the needle less scary."

"Interesting," he whispered. "It seems that human beings find ways to enrich their lives through visual stimulation. That must be why art is held in such high esteem amongst your people."

"Yes," I nodded. "Art has many forms that are not visual; there's also music, writing poetry, or novels."

"You mean typing?"

"Well, you can type stories or sonnets. But I think there's something to be said for lovely handwritten sentiment."

"Handwriting seems demeaning," he wrinkled his nose.

"How so?"

"It seems pointless to do something that requires more time and energy when superior methods and technology are readily available."

"Time and energy are what makes a handwritten love letter so precious."

"I do not understand."

"There's something special about taking the time and putting thought and care into each line and making every word a demonstration of your feelings for the person you're writing it for. It's become a lost art, even in my world. But I still feel that it's a priceless display of one person's affection for another."

He looked at me for a long time without speaking, then said, "I think human features are round and soft. I have always found looking at your face and body pleasant."

I could feel my forehead wrinkle, knowing that he didn't mean to come off so awkward. His attempt at complimenting me was sweet, even if he sucked at it.

"Thank you," I said with a smile.

"Did I say something wrong?" he frowned.

"No," I shook my head. "I guess it's just strange to think that you've been spending all this time touching and seeing my body and I didn't even know it."

"If you are concerned about my honor, you should know that I would never…"

"No," I put my hands up. "I'm not concerned about that at all."

"I am a doctor and treat my patients with the utmost respect."

"Well, I appreciate that," I nodded. "Thank you."

"You are welcome," he stood and walked back to the panel where he got our drinks. "Would you like to eat something before the accelerant takes effect?"

"What happens when the accelerant takes effect?"

"You will feel tired and most likely fall asleep until you are well. Do not worry - there is still time to eat if you're hungry."

"Sure," I sighed, wishing he would tell me this stuff before injecting me with alien substances. "I would love something to eat."

"I have something that will help with some of the cravings you have likely been experiencing."

I bit my lip, thinking how unlikely it was that he could know what I had truly been craving the most. But not wanting to dampen his optimism, I simply changed the subject.

"So how did you become a doctor?"

He closed the panel and opened another one which contained some sort of brilliantly colored fruit tree. Picking two baseball-sized yellow fruits, he returned to the couch.

"I have been training to be a doctor since I was very young. My older brother and I both were intrigued by Earth and all the exotic species that are found there and nowhere else," he said and handed me one of the fruits. "I looked up to him very much. He was accepted into an educational program that involved field work and I was selected to go to the medical academy. I was happy for him, but I had negative feelings about his absence."

"You missed him," I stated, watching as he bit into the yellow fruit. He nodded at me as if to show me how it was done. When I bit into the crisp flesh of the fruit, my mouth was overcome with a warm sensation and a sweet-savory flavor.

"This is interesting," I said between bites. "Where is your brother now?"

"He was killed by two human males during a field expedition."

"Korin, I'm so sorry," I reached out and took his hand.

"You shouldn't feel sorry. You did nothing wrong."

I tried to think in the most literal terms that I could, then said, "Seeing your pain makes me feel pain. And my inability to make you feel better, makes me feel sorry."

"I think you are..." he searched my face, "kind."

I smiled and took another bite of the fruit.

"What is your assessment?" he asked, indicating with his eyes towards the fruit.

"It's strange at first, but very good."

"It has been extinct on Earth for a very long time. When the last ice age wiped it out, along with many other protein-based plants, most life forms turned to eating the flesh of other sentient beings to survive. I understand this is still a common practice on your world."

"Eating meat? Yes, I'm not sure the vast majority of Earth's population would be on board with giving up meat just yet. I was kind of forced to."

"Disgusting," he shuddered and looked away.

"Your race doesn't eat any kind of meat?"

"It is viewed as a serious crime in civilized society. Similar to murder and cannibalism on your planet. How can you not see the barbarism in taking the life of a creature capable of feelings, thoughts, and emotions, then desecrating and consuming their remains as if that matter had not just belonged to the body of another living creature?"

"I see your point," I nodded. "It's more of a habit than anything. Most of the meat produced in our world is grown from cultures in labs these days. But the wealthy still prefer the meat of once-living animals."

At this point, I became aware of my heart rate slowing. I unintentionally leaned toward him and rested my head on his shoulder. He reacted by putting his arm around me.

"The accelerant must be working even faster than I expected. When you've healed, you will wake naturally, and I will send you home."

I tried to respond and acknowledge what he said but I was fast asleep before I could open my mouth to speak.

When I opened my eyes, my first thought was that it had all been a dream. Upon taking in my surroundings and finding myself still on Korin's couch, I rubbed my eyes.

"I seriously can't get used to the fact that this is really happening," I said out loud to no one in particular.

Korin called out from another room, "Someone who has been studying the stars all their life is shocked to find that life beyond their home planet exists."

I followed the sound of his voice and found him seated at a desk looking at a large screen and scrolling through line after line of data.

"I *seriously can't* get used to the ignorance of your kind," he said without looking up.

His attempt at sarcasm was neither witty nor cute.

"You know what, I thought for a little while that perhaps I judged you too harshly, but I stand by my original assessment. You're a dick!"

"Is that another figure of speech?" he said, turning to look at me.

"You speak modern English. I know you know what a dick is."

"Indeed, but I fail to understand why it is an insult."

"Oh, for fuck's sake."

"I understand why *asshole* is used as an insult."

"I'd really like to go home and commence forgetting about this whole thing."

"Very well," his expression seemed more offended at my wanting to leave than at my calling him names.

"Here's your teleport rock thingy," I held out the silver stone to him. "I won't be needing it anymore."

"You'll need the orb to get home," he said, then turned back around to focus on whatever data was on his computer screen. "Leave it in plain sight in your quarters and I'll have an assistant pick it up as soon as possible."

"So, I just close my eyes and picture my bedroom and I'll be home just like that?"

"Something like that," he said, not bothering to turn back around to look at me.

"Well, I wish I could say it's been a pleasure," I said clutching the stone to my chest. I closed my eyes and visualized standing in my bedroom. When I opened my eyes, I was greeted by a dark room. Walking into my living room I called out to my smart-home A.I.

"All lights on!"

69

When the lights came on, the first thing I noticed was the massive pile of mail that had collected beneath my mail-slot.

*How long was I gone?*

# Chapter
## FIVE

"House, what is the date and time as of now?" I asked loudly.

Ordering my A.I. around wasn't something I usually did but I didn't want to have to find my phone before getting to the bottom of this. The A.I. responded, telling me the time right down to the second. I sank to my knees. Almost a week had passed.

*Deep breaths Natalia, deep breaths.*

I walked to the restroom and sat down to pee. I certainly didn't feel like I had been holding my bladder for a week. I washed my hands and looked for where I had flung my purse when I got home the last time I had been here, panicking over my bioluminescent blood. I found it in the hall closet, crumpled as though I had tossed it in there hurriedly. I fished out my phone, which was unsurprisingly dead.

After charging it for long enough to switch it back on, I saw 49 missed calls and 27 voicemails displayed on the screen. The first one was from Laura asking if I was alright. The next two were from Mom whom I usually called at least a couple times a week to check in. Next, Abiola called and said that my department manager was getting angry that the project hadn't been completed. Then a few more from Laura and Abiola telling me that they showed up at my house and used Laura's emergency key to make sure I wasn't passed out somewhere but found nothing. The next message was Laura in tears, explaining that she and Abiola had gone to the police and reported me missing and that if I wasn't dead or kidnapped, I'd have a lot of explaining to do.

The police had called notifying me that I was reported as a missing person and to contact them immediately when I received their message. The remaining messages were all from Mom, Laura, and Abiola... sometimes drunk or crying or both just telling me that they loved me and to please be okay.

It would have been heartwarming if I wasn't panicking over how I was supposed to piece my life back together after going missing for a week. I decided that the first call needed to be to the police. I didn't want them wasting their resources trying to find me when there might be someone else out there that actually needed their help. I pushed the call back button and hung my head like I was a prisoner waiting to be executed.

"Detective Ra'az," a raspy voice answered.

"Hello, my name is Natalia Winters... I just discovered that my friends reported me missing some time in the last few days."

"Yes, Miss Winters," his voice lifted as if he was happy to hear from me. "Your mother and two friends have been really worried about you. Are you injured?"

"No," I bit my nails.

"Are you or were you being held against your will?"

"No, sir."

"Are you in need of police assistance?"

"No, thank you. I'm sorry for worrying everyone."

"May I inquire as to your whereabouts since last Tuesday?"

"I'm not actually sure. I seem to have blacked out."

"Do you require medical attention?"

"I'm going to see my doctor first thing tomorrow."

"Well, while you're out and about, please come by the station in person and bring your identification or smart-band so that we can verify that you're safe and accounted for."

"I'll come by as soon as I get out of my doctor's appointment."

"Sounds like a plan. Glad you're okay."

"Thank you. Goodnight."

I hung up the call then rubbed at my forehead as I pondered how my next phone calls were going to be. I found my mother's phone number and pressed *call*.

"Nattie?" Her voice sounded hoarse, probably from crying.

"Yeah, it's me. I'm so sorry for not calling."

"The police called me asking if I'd seen you and said that your friends had reported you missing! Where the hell have you been?" Her yells gave way to sobs and I felt like the world's biggest asshole.

"I don't know, Mom. The last thing I remember was walking to work. I started…" I stopped for a moment and chose my next words carefully, "having a panic attack or something. I turned around and ran home where I blacked out and I don't remember anything since then."

"I'm going to come to Las Vegas right now!"

"No, Mom," I pleaded. "I'm going to see my doctor tomorrow and I'm going by the police station. After that, I need to try and salvage my job if I haven't already been fired. I have a million things I have to take care of."

"I could stay with you for a bit. Just until your doctor is able to…"

"Mom! I said I'm fine. I'm just busy and I don't need you hovering over me while I'm trying to get back on track."

I didn't realize how cruel I sounded until I stopped talking and sat there breathing in silence as she formulated her reply.

"Alright, sweetie. I didn't mean to stress you out even more. I've just been really scared that something awful must have happened to you."

"As far as I can tell, I'm fine. Not even dehydrated. So, wherever I was, I'm pretty sure I was eating and drinking and staying out of the elements."

"Well, I'm relieved you're okay. Call me tomorrow. Please? After your visit to see the doctor and let me know how you're doing."

"Will do, Mom."

"Okay, I love you, Nattie."

"Love you too, Mom," I tried to adopt a gentler tone. "Goodnight."

The next call was to my doctor who was able to fit me in for an early morning appointment, for which I was grateful. I didn't feel the least bit tired. After all, I had just woken up from a seemingly very long nap.

Laura and Abiola were understandably peeved and told me that I had better bring a doctor's note when I came back to the office. I had no problem doing that. For all I knew, I really was suffering from some sort of psychosis and hallucinated the whole thing. I went to my basement and pulled out some old paintings from when I first got really sick. It was the only time in my life that I had felt compelled to paint human figures. I pulled out a crate of protective tubes containing my rolled-up canvases and carried them upstairs. Each canvas was about two feet tall and four feet wide.

I pulled the lid off the first tube and unrolled the painting onto the floor. A familiar face stared up at me; Korin with his flawless blue-tinted skin and gentle eyes. I hadn't drawn and painted these from memory. I had simply attempted to paint an image I had conjured up from my own imagination, or so I thought. Korin had said that the anesthesia made me forget. Maybe, my subconscious remembered him when he first started treating me.

As I opened the remaining paintings, there was little doubt in my mind. Either it was all real and some part of me knew and remembered this man, or none of it was and I was experiencing a full-on psychiatric break that had been a full year in the making. Logic told me that the latter was more possible. But when I strained to remember my experiences with sleep paralysis, piecing together what Korin had told me was actually going on, I couldn't help but believe that he was real. I supposed there was only one way to find out.

When I got to my doctors' office, I signed in and waited patiently in the lobby. It was only a few minutes before Dr. Wang's nurse called me in. They weighed me and took all my vitals. When the doctor finally entered the room, she smiled warmly and put on her latex gloves.

"How are you feeling, Natalia?"

"Physically, I'm feeling alright. But I'm having some pretty serious blackouts and I need to put a stop to it."

"Blackouts?" she frowned and picked up her tiny funnel-shaped flashlight to look in my ear. "What kind of blackout are we talking about?"

"Last Tuesday I was walking to work, and I started feeling off. I was seeing lights that didn't make sense, so I went home and the next thing I knew, a week had passed, my mom and friends were freaking out, and I was reported as a missing person. I'm not even sure if I have a job to go back to at this point."

"Have you had an issue with attendance at work in the past?"

"No. Never."

"Then I'm sure your employer will work with you to move forward after this. I'm going to give you a note excusing your absence for the week. I would suggest staying home until we can run a full panel of tests and figure out what's happening. I'll get you in as soon as I can. I'll have my nurse let you know when to come in. It shouldn't be more than a couple of days for an appointment prompt. If you can't make it, you will be placed on a waitlist for any subsequent openings, okay?"

"That sounds good. Thank you."

The receptionist printed out a note excusing me from work for the past week and I was able to reach the police station just in time to catch Detective Ra'az who was an older Hispanic man with broad shoulders and a salt and pepper beard.

"How was your doctor's appointment?" he reached out and shook my hand. He was a tall sturdy looking man.

"It went alright. I have to go in for a bunch of tests before I'll be able to get any answers, but that's to be expected."

"That makes sense," he stroked his beard and took his mobile device from his pocket to scan my smart-band and process me out of the missing person's data-base. "Stay in touch and say hello to your mother for me."

His final statement took me by surprise, not because I didn't know he had spoken with Mom, but because of how he said it. I couldn't help but get the feeling that he actually wanted me to tell my mother that he said hello.

My last stop for the day would be OSA. My depart-ment manager would no doubt be in and I needed to explain myself and throw myself at his mercy. Hope-fully, my doctor's note would give my story some cred-ibility in his eyes. But the truth was that, even if I had a medical reason for not calling or showing up for an entire week, it wouldn't remove the need for someone to do my job. If I was unable to do that, my top-rated status would be dissolved, and I would have to go back to the bottom of the corporate food-chain when and if I was able to return.

"Good afternoon, Miss Winters," came the A.I. greeting. It was so formal, even using my last. It wasn't a good sign.

"Good afternoon," I responded regardless.

I took the elevator straight to the sixth floor where Mr. Andrews' office was waiting. The offices on this floor didn't have the same transparent walls as floors four, five and six. This was where the hiring, firing, and everything in between went down. The ceilings were high and the corridors wide, but I still felt suffocated walking to what felt like the end of my career.

The office at the end of the hall had a placard that read 'C. Andrews, Department Manager'. The door was open, so I peered in and knocked gently on the open door.

"Miss Winters," he looked up from his smart desk that had eliminated the need for paper documents. The entire top of the desk was a touch screen with access to all documents related to our department. I had always wanted a desk like this, but it was still above my paygrade, especially now. "I'm glad to see that you're alright."

"Thank you, sir," I said, handing him my doctor's note.

"You've been off sick?"

"No, sir," I stammered. "Well, yes, sir."

"It says here that your doctor wants you to stay home until further notice."

"I would still like the opportunity to work from home if you're open to me using my personal tablet for the Lunar Resort project."

"Actually, I had Jen complete the Lunar Resort project," Mr. Andrews scratched his head.

"Oh," I felt my cheeks burning. Jen was a mediocre artist who got where she was through sheer likeability rather than talent and hard work.

"There are a few less pressing projects that are for articles that won't be due for another month. I will allow you to take your work tablet home if you can provide me with updates daily, or at least every three days or so. Can you commit to that?"

A ray of hope lifted my spirits and I agreed quickly. "Yes, sir."

"If your medical condition worsens and you aren't able to fulfill your obligations, I need you to understand that I need to place someone dependable in your position permanently. You won't get fired, but I'll need to put you somewhere, where your limitations won't affect the company."

"I completely understand, sir," I said, my voice wavering. "I love this company and I've worked really hard to get to where I am. I'll do everything in my power not to let you down."

"That's good to hear, Miss Winters," he placed my doctor's note face down, allowing his desk to scan it into his files before handing it back to me.

Taking the glass elevator down, I pushed the button that would take me to the fourth floor where I could collect my work tablet and see Laura and Abiola. As I slowly descended, I could see through the glass that Jen was sitting at my desk and Laura was standing beside her holding out her hand. Jen took Laura's hand to inspect the back of it and, as I looked at the overjoyed expression on everyone's faces, I suddenly realized what was happening. Alex had proposed. I quickly pushed cancel on the elevator pin-pad and pressed the button for the first floor repeatedly. Laura looked up just in time to lock eyes with me as the elevator moved past the floor.

Damnit! Now she was going to know that I purposely avoided her. I backed against the wall and fought back tears. Of course, she was getting married. She and Alex worshiped each other. I wanted her to be happy, so why did this hurt so badly?

Hyperventilating, I clenched my fists and suppressed the urge to scream. As soon as the doors opened, I raced across the lobby, not acknowledging the A.I.'s courteous farewell. I was hurting because I knew I was losing the only people in my life that cared about me, and it was no one's fault but my own. Abiola and Trevor would get married this spring. Laura and Alex would probably not be that far behind... And I would still be here, alone, struggling with an illness I didn't understand and with the new addition of what might be a psychotic breakdown. The tears were now streaming unbridled down my face as I walked home.

Even the job that I had made the sole focus of my entire life was being taken out from under me by *Jen* of all people. Jen who couldn't compose a decent painting to save her life. She would probably be a bridesmaid at Laura's wedding. I would just see pictures on social media platforms that I don't even have a profile on anymore because I hated talking to people. The worst part was that Jen was actually a really nice person. She might be a less than spectacular artist by my standards, but I had no real problem with her as a person except that she was stealing my job and my friends. I would be stuck working from home on projects that didn't matter, and I would grow old all alone and never even get to see outer space.

*Perhaps, I'm being a little overdramatic, but still, ugh!*

My memory drifted back to the moment I looked out the window of Korin's ship. The beautiful, greyish-blue not-so-perfectly round planet that everyone else would

only ever see in bright artificial colors. I got to see it…
once. At least I got to see it once.

Around 11:00 PM that night I decided that I should
probably go back to my desk and retrieve my work tablet while none of my coworkers were there. How was I
ever supposed to face them again after how I had acted?

"Good evening, Miss Winters."

"Good evening," I answered the A.I., irritated to find
that it was still using my surname.

When I reached the third floor, I was less than delighted to find Jen working late. I almost turned right
back around and left, but I needed my tablet.

"Oh, Natalia!" she perked up and waved, "Mr. Andrews put a memo in the system, giving you clearance
to take the tablet home."

"Yes, that's why I'm here actually."

"I was just staying late to look at the custom digital
brushes you made. I was trying to notate all the specifi-
cations so that I could use them on the Martian Terra-
forming concept paintings."

Nice. She's even stealing my brush designs.

"I'll put them into a file and send them over to you
in the next couple days," I responded with what I knew
were clipped tones, but I couldn't help it. I reached out,
waiting for her to hand the tablet over.

"That would be such a big help," she sighed. "I feel like I'm in way over my head trying to fill your shoes. When will you be back?" she asked, placing it gently in my outstretched hand.

"I don't know. Soon, I hope."

"Thank god," she let out a nervous giggle. "I always wanted the chance to work with you. I'm a huge fan of your work."

I wanted to hate her for being a fake vindictive bitch, but the truth was that she seemed completely genuine.

"You're sweet," I said over my shoulder as I walked away. "Have a good night."

"You too," she replied meekly.

When I got home to my empty house, I closed the door behind me and leaned against it as I slid to the floor. I didn't even bother turning my lights on. All I wanted to do was sit there in the dark and cry and scream until I had no voice left. But I couldn't even do that. At some point, after my dad didn't show up for the umpteenth birthday, I stopped expressing my true feelings. I just pushed them down into the darkest part of myself and ached quietly, waiting for the pain to subside.

I had always felt out of place in this world. But at that moment, I wanted more than ever to disappear.

# Chapter

## SIX

Sitting there against my front door, I looked at the moon that was now visible through my floor to ceiling windows across the living room. This view was one of the main reasons I bought this house. The cool light filtered through the panes of glass and across the paintings that were still unrolled and scattered around the floor.

Forcing myself to stand, I walked through the foyer and into the moonlight, closing my eyes as it spilled onto my skin. I looked down at the painting of Korin's face. His deep nebulous eyes staring back at me, I felt a slight reprieve of my pain. I knew that even if he was real, the thought of any deeper connection with him was pure fantasy. Still, the weight of my loneliness was so much heavier than any consequences I could imagine.

I turned to look at my kitchen island and the silver stone that still sat there, waiting for me. I walked over and reached out to pick it up. I turned to stare once more out at the night sky and yearned for the peace I felt when I was with him. I didn't intend to travel back to him, but my desire to do so must have activated the stone, because I felt myself becoming translucent and moving upward, through my ceiling and out toward the night sky.

I could feel the cool air all around me as I ascended and I smiled into the darkness as I flowed, formless through the cosmos toward the strange otherworldly man who was risking his career, and possibly his freedom, to help me. Everything faded to black and when I opened my eyes, I was standing back in his quarters. I looked down, my work tablet was still in my other hand. I set it down on the couch and walked into his bedroom.

He was sleeping peacefully in his bed which was levitating about two feet off the floor. I knelt down and whispered as I touched his arm.

"Korin," I whispered uncertainly, hoping he wouldn't be completely freaked out that I came back uninvited.

When his eyes opened, I felt immediately at ease. His expression was gentle and, even though he didn't smile, I could tell he wasn't upset.

"Why did you come back?" he blinked. "You said you wanted to forget everything."

"I didn't mean it," I looked down. "Like you said, I've been looking at the stars all my life. Coming here, meeting you; it's been amazing. I just get overwhelmed sometimes."

"That is understandable," he said gently. He sat up and his blanket fell and exposed his lean muscular torso. "Your human psyche is fragile."

I looked away to hide my reddening cheeks.

"You really need to work on your people skills," I joked.

"If you are referring to what human physicians refer to as *bedside manner*, my patients are unconscious, requiring little to no interpersonal skills."

"I suppose you have a point," I shrugged. "I'm sorry for busting in on you when you probably have to rest before work."

"I do not have work for another 29 hours," he stood up, unashamed of his nudity, and walked to the wall panel that contained his clothes. "I will get dressed and make you something to eat."

"So, this is like your weekend," I said, averting my eyes and pointedly examining the rest of the room.

"Yes," he said. From the corner of my eyes, I could see that he was putting on what resembled a fitted t-shirt and what I supposed was the alien equivalent of pajama pants. "It is vital to maintaining a healthy mind and body to take regularly scheduled leave."

"I agree," I followed him to his living area. "Although, I probably work more than I should."

"Your job is painting," he stated.

"So?"

"You love painting."

"Yes, but I still have other things that I like to do."

"What things do you like to do?"

I tried to look away from his shapely pectoral muscles that were being hugged so perfectly by his shirt. I swear, I tried, but he noticed and looked down at his shirt as if to try and figure out what I was looking at.

"I like exercising. It looks like you do as well," I gestured to him.

"I exercise regularly, but I wouldn't say I enjoy it," he turned his attention to the wall panels. "I will cut up an assortment of vegetables from my planet so that we can learn your preferences."

"That's very considerate of you," I smiled and paced the length of the room, searching for some clue as to what kind of person he was when he wasn't shoving needles into unconscious women. "What do you like to do in your free time?"

"I enjoy reading," he opened a panel and took out something that looked like a furry cucumber and I tried not to look as grossed out as I felt.

"I love reading too. What do you read?"

"Historical documents and medical journals mostly," he opened another panel and there was a small tree whose fruit looked like tiny human hearts, beating and pumping complete with ventricles attaching the fruit to the branches of the tree.

"I would have a hard time getting through that kind of reading."

"Why?" he continued, while collecting the ingredients for his fruit and veggie tray.

"I suppose I'm just more interested in romance and science-fiction."

"You prefer to read things that aren't true, rather than to expand your knowledge of reality?"

"Absolutely!" I sat down on the couch.

"Here," he said tapping his foot to a square on the floor.

The square tile lifted from the floor and levitated at about the height of a bar stool next to the counter where he was preparing our meal. I waved my hand underneath it and he chuckled. I pushed down on it with my hand to find that it had inflated with some sort of gel-based cushion. Sitting down cautiously, I could see him trying to hide his amusement at my obvious ignorance of things he was accustomed to. I imagined it was probably similar to watching a caveman play with a light switch.

"I get to experience reality every moment of every day," I tried to pick up where we left off. "If I'm going to sit down and read something for enjoyment, I want it to be larger than life; adventure, danger, romance! That's what the average person longs to experience through fiction."

"The average person doesn't experience romance?"

"Well, I suppose some people do. But I don't," my shoulders slumped. "And when I do, it's horrible. In the novels I read, it's always epic and beautiful and there's always a happy ending."

"Tell me about your romance," he said, taking a sharp knife from one of his wall cubbies.

"You want to know about my love life?" I asked, feeling my forehead crinkle with curiosity.

"Is that inappropriate?"

"No," I shrugged. "I suppose not. Well, I had a boyfriend when I was 16." I folded my hands and leaned on the countertop. "He was a disgusting excuse for a human being."

"Then why did you choose to have a romance with him?"

"I was young, and I guess you don't always get to choose who you love. That's why they call it falling."

"Interesting," Korin's eyebrows drew together as he concentrated.

"He sat next to me in algebra class. One day, he told me that Natalia was a feminine version of Nathan, which was his name. He was tall and blonde with blue eyes and I thought he was the most beautiful boy that had ever lived. He knew exactly what to say to make me feel amazing. He would tell me how perfect I was. My self-esteem issues just made me an easy target for all his flattery."

"It was bad that he told you things that made you feel amazing?"

"Well, the bad thing was that he didn't mean any of the things he said," I explained. "And he wasn't always nice. If I didn't do what he wanted or if I did something he didn't like, he knew just what to say to destroy me."

"His words could destroy you?"

"Figuratively, yes. He would say things that made me wish I was dead like I was a horrible person and completely worthless and that I didn't deserve him."

"Why would he say things to make you feel that way?"

"To get me to do whatever he wanted."

"You did what he wanted because you wanted him to make you feel amazing. And he would destroy you to keep you subjugated to his will."

"Yes, exactly," I nodded, excited that he was able to understand where I was coming from. "That's how he got me to sleep with him, and once that happened, he had even more control because I didn't want to ever be with anyone else that way."

"Because you slept with him?"

"Well… not literal sleep."

"What is figurative sleep?"

"It's a figure of speech. It's kind of an outdated term, I guess, but to sleep with someone can refer to sexual intimacy."

"I see," he blinked. "So he manipulated you into engaging in intercourse because he wished to procreate."

"No," I laughed. "Does your species only have sex to procreate?"

"No, we often enjoy intercourse for pleasure as well as its various health benefits."

"Okay, not so different from us, then. I think humans prefer sex that doesn't result in pregnancy. I can't procreate anyway. I have a medical condition that took that off the table, which I'm okay with. I don't think I would be a very good mother. But the reason he wanted me to have sex with him was more of a power trip. He knew my emotional dependence on him would be even stronger if I had sex with him and he was right."

"I see," he furrowed his brow as he peeled the furry cucumber.

"I heard all the rumors going around about him sleeping with other girls but, whenever I confronted him, he made me feel guilty for not trusting him. Then, the day before prom, he dumped me for one of those girls, and I realized what a gullible idiot I had been for loving him so blindly."

He paused and set his knife down.

"Hearing you tell that story makes me feel sorry that I can't make you feel better."

I couldn't help but smile.

"That's sweet."

"Why does that please you?"

"I guess because your desire to make me feel better makes me feel better."

"Why?"

"Because I like you," I responded without thinking.

He pondered what I had said for a moment, then returned to his work, "What about after Nathan was no longer your prospective mate? Why did you not find a more suitable match?"

"I tried," I braced my elbow on the counter and propped my chin on my hand. "I wanted to fall in love with someone, but I also didn't want to be manipulated. You can't really let yourself get attached to anyone if you don't want to risk them hurting you."

"So, in romance, you have to expose yourself to danger in order to also expose yourself to happiness."

"Exactly."

"You read about fictional romance to experience artificial happiness so that you don't have to expose yourself to real danger," I didn't respond but simply evaluated what he was saying and realized that he wasn't far from the truth. "Now I understand the human psyche's need to read fiction."

I felt like this summary was an oversimplification of things, but I didn't really want to go into any further analysis since my brain was already straining to communicate on his level.

"So, what about you?" I gestured to him.

"Me?"

"Yes, tell me about the spicy alien lady that's waiting for you back on your planet."

He looked confused.

"Not literally spicy; I mean sexually desirable."

His expression relaxed and he nodded.

"I see. I have engaged in sexual activity with several prospective mates since I reached sexual maturity. I found their company outside of coitus to be unfulfilling, thus acknowledging a lack of compatibility. The relationships ended amicably and, on the rare occasion that circumstances allow, they are still willing to engage in sexual intercourse with no intention to procreate."

"How romantic," I chuckled.

"Since our first meeting, I have studied human voice inflections that convey sarcasm."

"That's probably a good thing," I glanced down.

"I tried to engage in sarcasm with you last time we spoke," he looked at me intently. "It seemed to make you angry."

"I'm sorry," I squirmed in my seat. "That was probably not your fault. I guess I don't have the best interpersonal skills either."

He handed me a slice of fruit and I accepted it. He spent a few minutes teaching me the names of all the different fruits and vegetables and I tried each one. Most of them I liked, although the little beating hearts I found unsettling, and some of the selections I didn't like at all.

"Do you like music?" I asked.

"I am familiar with the concept of various tones played in a specific sequence, usually in a repeating pattern. It doesn't sound like something that would interest me."

"I bet you're wrong," I said skipping over to my tablet which I had left on the couch. "I bet you're a classical guy."

I started going through the playlists that I had downloaded for work and selected my ever-beloved Cello Suite Number One in G Minor. At first, when it began playing, he tilted his head skeptically. He walked over and looked down at me as if he was more interested in my reaction.

"Close your eyes and don't think about the strangeness of it," I said, and reached up to cover his eyes with my hand. "What do you *feel*?"

He lifted his hands to my waist, then said, "I feel, confused."

"Okay, now just listen and let yourself get lost in it."

"I feel, *intrigued*."

"Okay, can you elaborate?" I removed my hand from his eyes and let it rest on his arm as he was still hanging onto me. "I want to know what you feel."

He opened his eyes and looked down at me and I admit I found myself completely taken in by his gaze. I swallowed and forced myself to take a calming breath.

"For example," I continued, "when I hear this song, I feel safe and wild. It makes me feel like I'm braver than I am. Like, if I wanted to, I could fall in love without being afraid."

"I thought you said you can't always choose."

"That's true," I took my hand off his arm and he let go.

We sat down together and listened to music for hours, talking about the artists that wrote the songs or who performed them. Watching his eyes as he listened to the lyrics, I was mesmerized by how enthralled he was; like a child seeing the ocean for the first time.

"I like the songs that reflected what was important to people at the time in which they were written," Korin said at one point, and scooted a little closer and started listing some of the bands we had listened to. "The Beatles, Bob Marley, Billie Holiday; they all used music as a means to express unpopular opinions."

"That's true," I nodded. "They used music to get people to listen to their thoughts and ideas. By reaching people on an emotional level, they were able to affect positive change on a massive scale."

"Human's being emotionally driven creatures controlled by their primal natures are more easily persuaded by these means?"

"I wouldn't say all people," I shrugged. "But some people that can't be reasoned with will lower their defenses when they're being entertained. It's what gives great storytellers the power to open people's hearts."

"By appealing to their emotions, the songwriters were able to open people's minds?"

Unsure of how to answer, I leaned in and kissed his lips softly. His eyes locked onto mine and his bewilderment faded into a gentle smile. He didn't speak, but we sat together long into the night until I fell asleep. When I woke up, I was covered with a blanket and he was gone.

I walked to his bedroom to find him sleeping with my tablet still playing through its song library. I wrung my hands, trying to work up my courage and made my way over to his bed. Climbing up onto the levitating platform, I carefully slipped under the blanket, curling up next to him and closed my eyes. I wasn't tired at all so when he brushed a strand of hair out of my face, I was grateful. I opened my eyes to find him staring back at me with an expression that made me feel things that I hadn't let myself feel since I was a teenager.

I reached up to hold his hand, pressing it softly to my cheek. I could sense the tension in his arm as I took his hand in mine, holding it up to inspect his palm and fingers. His fingernails were the same as a human's, but his fingerprints were strange. The lines looked more symmetrical than ours, like a mandala or a sacred geometric pattern. I rubbed my thumb over his fingerprint before releasing him, then scooted closer to him.

"Do all members of your species have colors in their eyes like yours?"

"Not all of us," he smiled. "It's actually considered a defect to have more than one color."

"I think it's beautiful."

He reached out and put his arm over me. I leaned forward to brush my lips softly against his before anxiously pulling back to gauge his reaction.

*Was kissing even a thing on his planet or was randomly putting my mouth on his making him feel awkward?*

He didn't seem as surprised as when I kissed him in the living room. Almost immediately, he lifted his head and enveloped my lips with his, kissing me so sweetly that it stole the breath right out of my chest.

My hands moved instinctively to run my fingers through his black hair. His hand slid down to the small of my back pulling me against him. His lips parted as he sucked my bottom lip and I responded, throwing my leg over his hip. I hadn't had a great deal of experience with men, but I have to say, I had never felt this level of chemistry with anyone.

His hand found my hipbone where he pressed his thumb sending a shockwave of sensation up my body. I moaned softly. He rolled me off my side and onto my back, and kneeling between my thighs, looked down at me hungrily. I wondered if human sexuality was something that he had studied at length in his medical training. He put his hands on my waist and traced his fingertips across the top of my pants, his eyes searching mine for permission.

I lifted my backside, allowing him to pull my pants down and he made quick work of peeling them off along with my panties, which he tossed aside. As he pulled his shirt off over his head, the sinuous muscles I had glimpsed earlier were suddenly bare before my eyes. I sat up, bracing myself with one arm as I ran my fingertips over his hairless blue-tinted skin. His chest and abdomen looked and felt exactly as you would expect of someone who had never consumed a carbohydrate in their life; firm, sleek, and defined.

He scooped me up in his arms, pulling me in to straddle him as he sat back. I put my arms around his neck and kissed him deeply, feeling his body react and harden against me. His gaze drifted to my breasts, which had somehow stayed covered in my spaghetti-strapped tank-top. He traced the line of my collar bone with his fingers and softly put his hand around my throat. I lifted my arms and his hands moved down to my waist. Running his hands up the inside of my shirt, he pulled it off over my head before leaning me back gently. He rocked forward, settling down firmly between my open thighs. His hands were warm as they passed over my nipples, exploring the terrain of my ribcage.

He looked down at me as if he was unsure and finally asked, "Do you want this?"

A thoughtful question deserved a thoughtful answer. I considered all the possible consequences. I was undoubtedly feeling an emotional connection to him, even knowing that *this,* whatever it was, had an expiration date. Surely, he would eventually have to go home, and I would be left behind. It was obvious that there was no way for this to end other than complete and utter heartbreak.

On the other hand, with Korin, I knew exactly where I stood. There wasn't a manipulative or pretentious bone in his body and his honesty, though brutal at times, made me trust him implicitly. If ever there was a time to give in and go against my better judgment, this was it. The back of my hand brushed over his chest and abdomen as I reached down the front of his pants and took his member into my hand.

"Yes," I whispered, unfastening the top of his pants. I did want this. I wanted for once, in my empty miserable life, to feel exactly as he was making me feel at that moment.

He pushed his hips forward, finding my slick entrance and slowly burying his full length into my core as I lifted my hips to better accept him. When he pulled my face toward his and kissed me so deeply, there was no room for doubt he was not new to the concept.

Of course, my logical mind knew that it was in his nature to be detached, but the way he kissed me made me forget what I knew and believe that this was something real. He braced himself on one hand and reached up to grab the headboard with the other, taking his time, stopping to grind against me between thrusts, working me up to the edge only to withdraw before I could climax. Sweat beaded up on every inch of my skin and my thighs quivered, begging him to end my suffering, but he wouldn't. In fact, he seemed to enjoy watching me struggle.

"Please," I didn't mean to say it out loud, but he smiled, knowing exactly what I wanted.

He devoured my lips and neck with kisses, adopting a faster rhythm, working my body into a chemical frenzy. When he finally decided to push me over that delicious edge, he let go of the headboard and very deliberately took a handful of my hair and gently bit my earlobe as if only to feel the click of my earring against his teeth. He groaned into my ear as my body tightened around him over and over. I surrendered and let out a long, satisfied breath. He kissed my neck and laid down next to me, taking me into his arms.

"You're quiet," he said after a few minutes.

"I didn't want to be, but I figured it would be bad to make noise and get you in trouble."

"I meant, you haven't talked in a little while."

"Oh," I laughed softly "I guess you just wore me out."

"It's pleasurable to sit here with you quietly," he said. "However, I also enjoy our conversations."

"Thank you," I rolled over to rest my head on his chest and face him. "I like you too."

"I want to know more about you," he said. He brushed my hair back, causing a warm tingling sensation to ripple down the back of my neck.

"It's your turn to tell me something I don't know."

"Dinosaurs and humans coexisted."

"That's… actually really cool, but I want to learn about you," I said with a laugh. "Tell me about your home planet. Can you teleport there like I teleport here?"

"This ship is in Earth's orbit. The travel ore can only work over relatively short distances. My home is very far from here."

"Like, how far?"

"There is a portal about one million miles from Earth. It would take an hour traveling at top speed toward the constellation, Auriga, to reach the portal. Once through the portal, it would take another three hours to reach Miez."

"Miez? Is that the name of your planet?"

"Yes."

"What's it like there?"

"The ground is mostly light gray in color. There is an abundance of deep canyon systems filled with cities. Although the very highest elite citizens live on the surface. There is a great variety of plant life that thrives everywhere. Every part of our planet is covered with fresh water. Rivers and waterfalls are practically everywhere you go."

"What are your people like?"

"Our average people appear tall to your people. The color of Miezen skin varies much more than that of humans, although we all have a blue tint over whatever other color we happen to be."

"Are people divided by the colors of their skin?" I lifted my head and looked at him.

"No," he shook his head. "That is one of the most bizarre human customs."

"I can't say I disagree," I replied, and lay my head back down on his chest. "Do you guys have any special powers like mind reading or flying?"

"We can't fly, but we are able to share images with one another through a telepathic language. It's deliberate, like speaking out loud. We send messages to one another in the same way that we speak. We cannot *read minds*."

"What about your parents?"

"It is your turn," he said, with the rise of an eyebrow. "I have already shared a great deal of information about my home planet."

"Fair enough," I sighed. "My dad is an asshole. He left my mom when I was a baby. He used to call me a couple times a year and send me a present every year on my birthday."

"Did his life expire?"

"No," I smiled at his odd verbiage. "He's alive as far as I know. He still calls but I don't answer."

"Because he is an asshole?"

"Because I don't want him to just pop into my life whenever he feels it's convenient. He was never around when I needed him as a kid, and it hurt every time he acted like he gave a shit when he clearly didn't."

"And your mother?"

"She's a good person. I actually was kind of a jerk to her..." My jaw dropped as I suddenly realized that I had just screwed up badly again. "I was supposed to call her! I have to go home."

"Very well. I will have to be at work soon anyway."

"Wait, how long have I been here?"

"About 27 hours."

"Shit! How is that possible?" I jumped up and started searching for my clothes. "I haven't eaten properly since I first got here and I'm just now starting to get hungry."

"Miezen food is more nutritious and metabolizes more slowly."

"I'm not even tired."

"You slept in the lounge earlier."

"My tablet is still charged, and I didn't bring a charger."

He just looked at me like he wanted to say, "*Really*?"

"What? Do you have a tablet charger somewhere around here?"

"The ship itself is an infinite wireless power source."

"Oh, come on!" I found my pants and started rushing to get them on. "You can't have expected me to know that."

"You are right," he said. He got up and started getting dressed.

I found my travel ore and grabbed my tablet. I wondered if it would be awkward to kiss him goodbye. Deciding I didn't care, I walked up and kissed his cheek.

"I had a good time. Thank you for your hospitality."

"You are welcome," he replied, touching his cheek where I had kissed him.

With that, I held onto the ore, closed my eyes, and imagined my living room.

# Chapter
## SEVEN

I rushed over to the floor by my front door where I had left my purse. Fishing out my phone, I saw calls from my mother, Laura, my doctor and one from a number I didn't recognize.

*One thing at a time*, I told myself, pressing the call button over my mom's avatar. *Shit! Every time I go back to the ship, it's like I completely forget that I have a life down here. How could I be so stupid?*

"Natalia Elizabeth! Where have you been?" Mom only used my full name when I was in serious trouble.

"I'm sorry, Mom. I'm okay. I just forgot to call, and I left my phone in a weird place," I rushed to get the words out, but my throat tightened. "Please don't be mad."

"Well, I'm angry, but since you've already disappeared for a week before and turned up at random, I assumed you were alright this time too."

"Also," I changed the subject, "when I went by the station, Detective Ra'az told me to tell you he said hello."

"He's a sweet man. He was so kind and patient when I was a complete basket case, thinking you were kidnapped or dead."

112

"He's kind of handsome. Did you guys spend a lot of time together last week?"

"Well, no," she stammered. "It's just that I was coming in every day to make sure they were doing their job looking for you."

"Maybe you should call him and offer to make him dinner since you were a big pain in the butt last week."

"I was only a pain in the butt because I thought something happened to you!"

"Something did happen to me. I just can't remember what it was."

"Well, you were never the type to run off and party with some random guy," Mom said. "I knew it was something you had no control over."

"I love you, Mom," I said with more sincerity than I had in a long time. I looked at the paintings on my floor. "I'm sorry I'm such a grouchy jerk to you. I'm kind of a hot mess right now. But I'm going to get it together, I promise."

"Your voice is different. It's been a long time since you sounded this awake. Did you change your diet again?"

"Um, just trying to be healthy."

*She's used to me being evasive. She's not going to push it.*

Then a long dramatic gasp sounded through my phone speaker.

"Did you meet a guy?" she sounded like she was having a heart attack.

"Mom!"

"Or girl… I don't judge."

"I'm not a lesbian, Mom."

"So, you did meet a guy."

"No, mom," I lied through my teeth. "I'm just feeling better, but I need to get to work or I'm going to lose my job."

"You need to get out and meet people, sweetie. I don't want you to die alone."

"I'm an introvert. I enjoy being alone."

"Yes, but even introverts need to be alone with someone."

"That doesn't even make sense," I pretended not to know what she was talking about.

"Don't pretend you don't know what I'm talking about."

"Okay, I love you- bye!" I said, frantically ending the call.

The next phone call was to Laura. I messed up big time, and even after I hit the call button, I had no idea what I was going to say.

"Wow, you're alive…" she said, her voice sounding unimpressed.

"Yeah," I covered one half of my face with my hand in shame. "I can explain."

"You'd better."

"During the week I was missing, I don't know what happened," I said, deciding to stick to the same story I was telling everyone. "I blacked out and I didn't even realize a week had passed."

"Oh my god, Nattie!" her voice shifted from angry to concerned and I felt even more guilty for lying to my best friend.

"I saw my doctor who gave me a note and Mr. Andrews gave me a tablet to work on from home."

"Why didn't you call me as soon as you were awake?"

"I had to go to the police station and then I was going to talk to you when I got to work, but on the way out, I started having some kind of panic-attack-meltdown and I just... I'm sorry. I love you and I'm so sorry for everything. Please don't hate me."

"I could never hate you," she sighed. "You're my best friend and I want you in my life."

"I want to be there for you. I want to see you get married."

"Speaking of that," I could hear the smile in her voice, "Alex proposed!"

"That's so amazing," I put my hand over my heart. "I told you it was coming."

"I know!" she sounded like she was bouncing "You were right, he took me to a rooftop restaurant and got the DJ to play the song we danced to at my cousin Karen's wedding."

"The one you said you wanted as your wedding song?"

"Yes! And then the DJ got everyone to stop what they were doing for an announcement. Then he walked up to the table where we were sitting and said, 'Alex, do your thing man."

"No way!"

"And he stood up from the table, pulled the ring out of his pocket, and got down on one knee."

"No WAY!" I said even louder, feeling a genuine build-up to the punchline.

"And then the DJ held the mic so that everyone could hear. He said that ever since he met me, he's been happier than he ever thought was possible."

"Aw!"

"Then he said he couldn't imagine a future without me in it."

"Oh my god," my eyes clouded with tears.

"I'm sure he had a much longer speech prepared, but I tackled him to the floor and kissed the shit out of him."

"That sounds like you."

"He had the hostess record the whole thing on her phone and it's all over the internet."

"I bet you'll be internet famous for the next six months."

"I doubt it, but it was amazing."

"I'm so happy for you, Laura," I gushed. I genuinely felt elated as I imagined the scene she described playing out in my mind. There was still a dull ache when I thought about how that would never be me. But the weight of my loneliness wasn't nearly as intense as it had been a couple of days ago.

"Thank you! Oh, hey, Andrews has been asking about you. Did you get the art for those articles done?"

"I'm going to work on that right now. I have to call my doctor back first."

"Okay, well, call me later. I want to come over and show you some wedding dress designs. I need help."

"I might be hard to reach until I get caught up on the project Andrews gave me. But I'll call you as soon as I have time to hang out."

"Okay, don't forget about me!"

"I won't. I'll talk to you soon."

"Later, girl."

Looking at the dozens of voicemails in my inbox, a handful were from Dr. Wang's AI prompt system and one was from the number I didn't have saved. It was local but I didn't recognize it. I listened to my doctor's last message and she told me that she had an opening on this Friday at 3:00 PM from the waiting list I was placed on three weeks ago. I looked at my phone and saw that it was Friday 2:49 PM.

"Crap!" I grabbed my purse and ran out the door.

As I walked, I decided to go ahead and listen to the other message.

"Hi," began a familiar voice. "It's Nathan Hanway. Your mom is social media friends with me. She's been worrying about you lately and asked me to come check on you. I came by but you weren't home. Anyway, give me a call and let me know that you're okay."

*Fat chance, douchenozzle.*

*I can't believe my mom would resort to sending that dickhead to my house!* She was definitely going to get an earful as soon as I had time to calm down.

I got to my doctor's office 20 minutes after I was supposed to be there. I told the receptionist that I had blacked out again and just got her message. She took pity on me and went ahead and took me in for the appointment. I had to get into a hospital gown, lay down in this white tube, and keep perfectly still for about ten minutes while they completed a full body scan.

"Your doctor will give you a call as soon as she's able to look over your results," the nurse said before telling me I could get dressed.

I went home and put my nose to the grindstone on the project Mr. Andrews had given me. After a few minutes, I realized that I had been humming some of the songs Korin and I had listened to together.

"House," I said out loud. "Play songs from the top 100 chart of the 1960s."

The house obeyed and I lost myself in the grunt work, nodding happily to the music and forgetting that the more prestigious jobs were being done by someone else. I found myself staring at the travel ore that was sitting across my desk. I shook my head and tried over and over again to stay focused on my work. About six hours in, I started looking at the clock and wondering how long Korin's workday was. I nibbled on some almonds and apple slices while I added some extra color where it made sense. By then, I had abandoned humming and was now singing at the top of my introverted lungs.

What was I doing? This wasn't who I was. I wasn't some giddy little school girl who falls apart because she has a crush on some guy. But Korin was no ordinary guy, and he made me feel like I was never meant to be ordinary either. Maybe I wasn't as cynical as I had always believed. Maybe I was just waiting for the right man to come along. Whatever the case, all I knew was that I couldn't stop smiling and that every time I got up to stretch my legs, I felt like dancing.

I fell asleep at my desk only to wake up and pick up exactly where I left off. The sooner I got this done, the sooner I could go back and see Korin again. And if I was being honest with myself, that was literally the only thing I could think about. Only stopping briefly to eat or use the restroom, I managed to push through that second day. It was at least a week's worth of work completed in less than 48 hours. It wasn't my best work, but it was still better than half of what came out of our art department on a daily basis.

My job mattered less and less the more I thought about how big the universe actually was. I even dared to fantasize that maybe I could travel with him and leave all of this behind. Of course, that was ridiculous. I didn't even know if I could survive on his planet. A song came on that happened to be playing when Korin and I were making love the night before and I couldn't pretend to care about the task at hand for a second longer.

I saved the work I had done and attached it to an e-mail to Andrews, apologizing for how long it took for me to get it finished. I reached across the desk, grabbed the ore, held it close to my chest and closed my eyes.

The feeling of traveling by ore was always exhilarating, no matter how many times I did it. I felt like a river flowing through space and time. I knew what I was doing was reckless and irresponsible, but I didn't care. I could have lived my whole life, dedicating every ounce of energy to my job, but nothing I was working toward made me as happy as the night I spent with him.

I opened my eyes…

# Chapter
## EIGHT

I stood in silence for a moment then felt his presence. His arms enveloped my body from behind and he nestled his face into my hair.

"I was hoping you'd come back," his voice made any worry that I was still holding onto melt away. I turned to face him and put my arms around his shoulders.

"I missed you."

"Have you eaten?"

"Yes, I snacked while I worked on my painting."

"I just got home, so I need to consume something relatively soon."

"Can I help you prepare your meal?" I asked. "I'd like to learn."

"It is fairly simple," he smiled. "I can show you."

I turned some music on using my tablet and let it sit nearby on the counter. He showed me how to use the panels and harvest some small fruits without harming the plant. Together, we cut up a few different things, and by the time it was done, I was hungry and wanted to try what we had prepared.

"I have been studying various visual and performing arts of your people," he said as he cleaned the counter where we had eaten.

"Did you find anything interesting?"

"I learned about heavy metal music, musical theater, stage acting, street magicians, and dancing."

"Wow," I was impressed. "That's a lot of information to cover. Any one of those could be the subject of a month-long study."

"I wish to learn more about these subjects, but my spare time will be limited for a while. I will have a lot of work over the next few days."

"I have work to do, too. But I can use my tablet and do my painting while you're at work. Do you mind if I stay here so I can see you when you come home?"

He seemed to hesitate in answering and I quickly backpedaled.

"Actually, that's a stupid idea, I'm probably spending way too much time up here..."

"That is acceptable," he interrupted. "I fear it may be an unnecessary risk having you here. But..."

"But what?"

"I enjoy your company. And I find that our reckless behavior has made me feel..." he furrowed his brow as if looking for the right word.

"I think I get it."

A cello cover of a popular romantic song started playing on my tablet, causing a swell of bravery to well up in my chest.

"Come here," I hopped up and held my hand out to him.

He looked at me hesitantly before walking up close enough for me to pull him in and put my arms around my neck.

"What is this?" He asked.

"Just close your eyes and try not to think about anything but the music."

"I'd like to. But this feels uncomfortable."

"It'll pass," I assured him, and started moving slowly side to side.

He looked down at my feet and copied my movements.

"Put your hands on my waist," I instructed. "Now move your body to match the pattern of the music."

"Is this right?" he asked sounding concerned, then cracked a smile. "I feel foolish."

I stepped back, taking his hands in mine and lifted one arm to do a twirl. He copied me and I laughed.

"There you go!"

The song ended and the next one was more up-tempo. I wasn't usually a fan of dancing but Laura and Abiola insisted that I go dancing with them, so I had learned a few moves that worked for songs like this one. He looked at me, unsure of what to do next.

"Just keep stepping side to side and move your arms however you want to."

"I don't want to move my arms at all."

I stifled a giggle at his response.

"Focus on the music and see if you change your mind," I suggested.

He closed his eyes and swayed side to side for a moment before breaking into a series of movements that would have made Elvis proud.

"Wow! I think you're a natural."

"Really?" He said. "I feel ridiculous."

"You don't look ridiculous. Are you having fun?"

"I think I am. I am enjoying this."

The song ended and another slow song started, and we stood looking at each other. I wanted to kiss him, but I worried that I was coming on too strong. After all, I already asked him if I could stay at his place while he worked.

"I must get some rest," he said, finally breaking the silence.

"Me too. I'm exhausted," I looked at the couch.

"You are welcome to share my bed if you like."

I blushed, having hoped he would offer, and said, "I'd like that."

I took off my pants and left them folded on the couch. He disrobed and put his discarded clothes into some kind of laundry shoot before climbing into bed. I didn't question it since he was naked in bed the first time I dropped in on him unannounced. It must have been a common practice in his society to sleep naked. I opted to keep my shirt and panties on since he had said he needed rest and, if there wasn't at least one layer of separation between us, I wasn't sure I could just let him fall asleep.

The next few days were the happiest I could remember. I would use the ore to travel back to my house only long enough to check in with my mom and my boss. I also took an opportunity to grab my personal tablet and download movies, music, and audiobooks that I thought Korin would like. When Korin would come home, we only had a few hours together before he would need to sleep. The work I was delivering my boss was mediocre at best because I had become fixated on drawing and painting the alien fruit trees in Korin's climate-controlled wall cubbies. When I wasn't interested in a project it was hard to deliver high-quality work. I suppose that's true of any artist. Nonetheless, Andrews accepted my work and continued giving me crappy projects.

Visits to my own home became less and less frequent. In fact, the only time I went back was to check in with my mother so she didn't send people to break my door down. My favorite part of the day was when he would come home, and we would snuggle up in his bed and watch movies. He quickly developed an appreciation for the sci-fi genre, especially one particular television series from the 1990s that followed two FBI agents as they investigated strange occurrences.

I hated feeling him slip out of bed every morning... if you could call it morning. In outer-space it's always dark outside the windows so it always feels like night time. I still seemed to need a lot more sleep than he did, and I would often wake up to reach across the bed to find his side empty.

Laura was probably going to be furious that I hadn't gotten together with her to help plan her wedding. I felt horrible, but I didn't know how long Korin would be here and I didn't want to miss out on a single moment with him, knowing that he could be gone from my life forever at any moment.

I got out of bed and stretched while walking around Korin's place. I considered taking a trip home just to take a walk around the block. I hadn't felt the sun on my skin in what would have translated to several days. It was then that I heard a noise coming from out in the hall. I walked to the door and listened more closely.

*Screams...*

Not your normal the-neighbors-are-drunk kind of screams. I was familiar with those ones. I could still clearly remember the people who lived next door to us when I was a kid. My mom had called the cops more than once, thinking that they were going to kill each other. But this was different. It was recognizable as a woman's voice, but the screams made me think that she was either in unimaginable pain or facing the end of her life. As the wailing continued, I became increasingly nervous. I knew that this was some kind of hospital. Maybe she was injured. Maybe the Miezen doctors were trying to help her, but I had a hard time convincing myself of that due to the sound of it.

I pressed my ear to the doors which reacted to my touch and slid open. My heart was pounding. I knew I shouldn't leave Korin's quarters, but I felt like I'd hate myself if I didn't at least check whether the woman screaming was alright or, at the very least, being helped. I peeked cautiously into the hall to find the corridor dark and empty. Stepping out of the room, I crept toward the sound.

There was only one room at the very end of the hall whose doors were open. There was a light on inside. I tiptoed cautiously toward the open room and peeked inside. To my horror, there was a naked human woman strapped down spread eagle on a floating table with some sort of levitating pod with a large metal arm reaching between her legs. Blood bubbled out around the edges of where the machine plugged into her body, and as she turned to look at me, her eyes wide in horror, I could see blood pouring out of her mouth onto the floor. I decided that, whatever they were doing to this woman, it wasn't in the spirit of medical treatment.

My first instinct was to help her, but I just stood there, frozen. Even if I did run to her side, what could I possibly do? There was more blood coming out of her than I had ever seen in my life. I wasn't a doctor, but I knew that much blood loss could only mean one thing. She wasn't walking out of here alive.

I needed to get back to Korin's quarters and use my travel ore to get home before anyone saw me. I turned around to run only to find myself face to face with a tall turquoise man in a grey uniform. He looked down at me with a harsh scrunched expression and grabbed my arm and twisted, causing me to cry out in pain. Pulling me into the room where the screaming woman was strapped down, he backed me against another floating table and started tearing at my shirt.

"No!" I screamed, "Don't fucking touch me!"

His massive hand clamped down on my throat and forced me down on the table and he started barking orders in a strange language to someone in another room.

I fought as hard as I could, kicking and scratching with all my might. But three other doctors entered the room and helped him get every part of my body strapped down so tightly I couldn't hope to get loose. My legs were spread and secured so that I couldn't even bend my knees.

"Don't do this," I pleaded. "HELP ME PLEASE!" I wailed, but they continued working as though I hadn't made a sound.

Sharp floating instruments were used to cut the clothes off my body. One of the doctors grabbed a handheld device with a screen on it and started moving it over my abdomen.

"I'm not sick," I begged. "Please let me go home. There's nothing wrong with me."

Korin suddenly rushed in and started talking to the doctors in a language that didn't sound like anything I had heard in my life. The conversation seemed to get heated and Korin got fairly aggressive with the turquoise man who finally huffed and reluctantly let me go. Korin helped me up and put his hands on my shoulders as if to guide me out of the room. I followed his lead, tears now streaming down my cheeks.

We walked past the other woman who had stopped screaming and was now lying silent, her face still twisted in horror as her dead vacant eyes stared blankly at the ceiling. The floating pod had a window on the side. I glanced at it as I passed and saw what looked like a live moving fetus floating in blue fluid.

My stomach twisted into a knot.

*What was this ship, really?*

# Chapter
## NINE

My heart was still racing, and the edges of my vision kept going dark as I strained desperately, trying not to lose consciousness or to allow myself to go into shock. I stared at my feet as we walked down the dark hallway back to Korin's apartment.

*Deep breaths.* I told myself. *If you want to make it through this, you're going to have to keep your shit together.*

I tried to disconnect from the pure and unadulterated horror of what I had just witnessed. I tried to forget about the blood, about the screams, the frozen death-mask of pain and outright terror etched on that woman's face. I shivered, not because I was naked, not because the hallway was a good ten degrees cooler than the inside of Korin's apartment, but because the logical side of my brain was starting to analyze the facts.

The *machine* that was hooked into that woman had sucked her baby right out of her womb. The doctors that just manhandled me, strapped me down and stripped me naked didn't seem the slightest bit interested in saving her. When they pinned me down, the only thing they seemed interested in was scanning me.

As soon as the door to his quarters slid shut behind us, I fell to my knees, unintentionally playing through the last few minutes in my head. The desperate screams, the sick squelching sound as the blood gurgled around that mechanical arm, the smell of metal and blood, the widening crimson pools on the chrome-colored floor. All my senses were overwhelmed, even the ones I couldn't decipher. Bile burned my throat as my stomach retched and I vomited onto the floor.

"What the hell is this place?"

Korin ignored my question and rushed to retrieve a towel to clean up the mess. His calmness, his meticulous focus on cleaning and dumping the dirtied towel had me reeling.

"Korin?" I persisted, "Why aren't you answering me?" Yet the silence lingered.

Every moment that passed thereafter, I began to realize that there was no answer that he could give me that would change what had just happened.

He opened his mouth to speak but reconsidered it seemed, fidgeting and straightening his shirt before heading toward the bedroom. Then changed directions twice before settling over the kitchen counter, exuding a feigned coolness, as if nothing was amiss. The spasms in my stomach caused me to gag and throw up again.

He rushed to his room and opened the panel that contained stacks of his folded clothing.

"Explain Korin!" I yelled. "Tell me again how this ship is... is here to treat humans for PARASITES!"

He cautiously knelt down beside me and held out a stack of folded clothes. He swallowed hard, stood up and glanced away, as if unsure of what to say next.

"KORIN!" I haphazardly threw the shirt over my head. My hands shook as I fumbled my way into the pajama pants. I desperately scooped his face into my hands.

"Nata-" His eyes darted away.

*I'm so fucking stupid.*

"I trusted you," I barely squeaked out. "You were lying the whole time."

"When I lied to you, I was trying to spare you from unnecessary distress."

"Tell... Me..." I locked eyes with him. "The truth."

"Very well," he pressed his lips together, took a deep breath and stepped away. "The ship we are currently on board is a breeding ship, whose sole purpose is to create the hybrid race that will one day replace humans as the dominant species on Earth. The women who are chosen as incubators cannot survive the extraction process. Natural birth does not occur. Rather, the fetus must be harvested."

# CHAPTER NINE

*What the hell is he talking about? Incubators? Harvesting?*

"Unfortunately, the human body is unable to separate from the Miezen placenta without severe and fatal hemorrhaging."

*That woman, the blood-*

"Eighty-seven percent of all incubators remain heavily sedated and completely unconscious during all procedures, including extraction."

*Now I understood.*

"The others have a high tolerance for the anesthesia and remain semi-conscious during the procedures. During the extraction process, the adrenal gland becomes highly active, causing incubators with a tolerance for the anesthesia to become fully aware. A more potent sedative would risk damage to the infant, so nothing can be done to ease their suffering."

I closed my eyes feeling rivers of warm tears streaming down my cheeks. Slow realization dawned with a cold sinking feeling that made my entire body shake.

"Korin," I paused, hoping he would know what I was trying to ask.

"You were selected to become an incubator a little over one year ago…"

"I'm pregnant."

"I am sorry."

"All this time I thought I was sick, but it was something you did to me," my legs shook. "Why?"

"When I extracted the nanobots, I began to process you out of the system as deceased. The plan was to terminate the pregnancy and let you live the rest of your natural life, never having known the danger you had been in."

"Why was I chosen?"

"That seems inconsequential."

"Come on, Korin," I shook my head. "Don't stop being honest with me now."

He tugged the bottom of his shirt to straighten it, just like he always did when he was nervous.

"Potential incubators must be sexually mature but not past the bloom of healthy childbearing years. The system selects them based on a low probability of procreating and... and whose disappearance would have a minimal impact on their family and the society in which they operate."

"I see," my gut tightened. I knew it. Unlovable. They had chosen me because the world would hardly notice that I was gone. I thought about the last few weeks and how my boss had so easily replaced me, about how the detective and my mom and a couple of my coworkers were the only ones to even wonder what happened.

"I am sorry," Korin folded his hands.

"…Okay," I said stepping further away. I noticed the blue sheen under his skin and the uncanny way he folded his arms.

*A stranger, I had let a complete stranger in.*

"I can terminate the pregnancy next time there is an open operating room," Korin explained. "All the sensors are out of your body and I can do the procedure in the next four hours."

"I need to get out of here," I said, and rushed over to pick up the ore and my tablet. My head was spinning, and I felt like I was having a heart attack. I had been through enough panic attacks to know I wasn't actually dying. But I wanted to have my meltdown in the safe, secluded fortress that was my bedroom.

"Time is running out, Natalia," Korin grabbed my arm. "The longer we wait, the more complicated the termination will be."

"Get your hands off me!" I scowled at him and wrenched my arm out of his grip.

Backing away I held the ore to my chest and imagined myself back in my bedroom. I didn't look at him. I don't even know if he heard the, "Goodbye," whispered under my breath just before I felt myself dematerialize.

The familiar smells of my clean house brought a strange comfort, but I knew that disaster was barreling toward me and I didn't have the emotional tools to cope with any of it. I took a moment to think about how much my illness had isolated me from everyone and everything. How many missed opportunities for normal relationships had come and gone without me ever even knowing it?

I went straight to my bed and pulled the covers over my head, even though I knew that sleeping wouldn't solve anything. But all I wanted was an escape and since a drinking binge was off the table, assuming I wanted to preserve the life growing inside me, my only option was to put myself into a depression-induced coma and await my tragic end.

I knew none of this was my fault. No one in their right mind would blame me for ending this nightmare and moving on with my life. But I couldn't help but wonder if that's what I even wanted. Hours passed and I lay there with my eyes closed, wishing I could sleep, but I couldn't. I pressed my fingertips gently at first, then firmly in a few different abdominal regions, trying to find anything that felt different, then I remembered. I wouldn't be able to feel anything. The thought crossed my mind that maybe this was all some insane hallucination or nightmare. Maybe I was in the middle of a legitimate psychological break and none of it was happening. As much as I wanted to believe that none of what I had just experienced had been real, I knew better.

# Chapter
## TEN

I woke up to the sight of the sun filtering in through the skylights. My phone had a ridiculous number of missed calls and the mountain of mail beneath my mail slot was bigger than ever.

Over the following days, my ex-boyfriend Nathan persisted in calling, texting, and leaving voicemails, which I consistently ignored. For a while, Laura and Abiola sent me an overwhelming number of get-well cards, flowers, balloons; you name it. My short, concise replies soon caused them to dwindle off. It made me sad, but at the same time, I intended to withdraw from the people who loved me the most. I figured that my eventual disappearance would be easier for everyone if I gradually lost touch first. I had mostly decided that it would be best to die.

Detective Ra'az would probably conduct a full investigation. Maybe he could help my mother through the grieving process. Perhaps they would date and eventually get married. She would never really get any closure. It would take two years for my insurance to pay out after my disappearance. Luckily, I paid for a ten-year policy only five years ago. It was reassuring to know that my mom would be taken care of for the rest of her life.

The only positive side to any of this was that I finally let myself unwind. There was no concern about my future because I didn't have one and there was a morbid freedom in knowing that. I took full advantage of my sound system and listened to music for hours. I had all my groceries delivered and binge-watched all the movies and shows I had missed over the last decade while I was busy being a responsible adult.

I stretched a canvas onto a wood frame and started painting. What ended up coming out was my interpretation of what I imagined a Miezen landscape to look like, the lush valleys that Korin described and some of the plant life that I had seen in his kitchen. Afterward, I felt a sick resentful rage building up just from looking at the damn thing. I took it out to my backyard and tossed it over the patio railing, where it could lie there in the grass and get sun-bleached for all I cared.

"House," I said aloud. "Play metal."

The house turned on a metal station and I kept telling it to play louder and louder until I could feel it vibrating through my skull and chest. I sat on the couch. Nathan was the only person who didn't seem to get the hint that I was trying to disappear. While everyone else called less frequently, he would call or text me every single day at the same time. I started to look forward to 10:00 PM, only because his kind words, however ill-intended they might have been, were the only comfort I had for almost two weeks following the discovery of my looming demise.

The one thing that I couldn't drown out, no matter how loud I blared my music, was the loneliness. It wasn't that I wanted sex. Believe me when I say that that was the last thing on my mind when I finally broke down and answered Nathan's call. It was the fact that I was lonelier than I had ever been, and I just wanted the briefest relief from that emptiness. I sat at my kitchen table at 9:48 PM and waited for my phone to ring. When it did, I wasn't quite sure what I planned to say; just that I was going to answer this time.

"H… Hello?"

"Holy shit," he suppressed a laugh with the words. "It's about time you answered your phone."

"Well, it was obvious that if I didn't, you were just going to keep calling."

"I apologize if it came off stalkerish. I swear, I'm not trying to make you uncomfortable. I just wanted to hear your voice once and know for myself that you're okay."

"I see."

"So, are you?" he asked. "Okay, I mean. Are you okay?"

I wanted to tell him the truth, but I figured he was probably just being polite so, instead, I said, "Yes, I'm fine. Just taking some time off."

"That sounds cool," he said lightly, then he began to worm his way in the way he always did. "It's been such a long time since we hung out. Since you have so much time on your hands, this would be the perfect time for us to catch up."

"I don't think that's such a great idea," I shifted my weight in my chair. "I know you're married, and I don't really think it would be appropriate for us to spend time together."

"That makes sense, and I understand why you feel that way," he responded. He sounded so sincere and I really wanted to buy it. "It's just that I've carried a lot of guilt about how I treated you when we were together and especially how it ended. I just want a chance to apologize face to face. If you don't want to see me, I'll understand and stop calling. I'm trying to grow past who I was and be a better person, but it's been hard considering I never got a chance to make amends for what I've done."

"Wow," I chewed my thumbnail. "That seems kind of out of character for you."

"I know," he sighed. "I don't blame you if you tell me to go fuck myself. I deserve it. But I had to at least reach out. After all the horrible things I've done, I needed to give it my best shot."

"Okay," I leaned forward and put my elbow on the table. If I could offer him some closure and help him be a better person before I shed my mortal coil, then why not? I figured I could use all the good karma I could get. After all, it was now or never, and who was I to deny him a chance to apologize for what he had done?

"Okay, what?"

"Okay, you can come over tomorrow," I swallowed. "But only for a few minutes."

"I get off work at ten - will that be too late?"

"I have nothing but time," I lied, not knowing exactly when my life would end. If it was meant to be, I would still be around to hear his bullshit apology.

Part of me just wanted to break up the monotony of it all. I wanted someone to talk to and I wasn't about to go back to Korin's ship, knowing what goes on up there. This would be a nice final goodbye to the trauma of my past before moving on to my next life.

I brushed my hair up into a messy bun and threw on some mascara, but made the conscious decision not to shave my legs. Nathan was, after all, my ex-lover. I wanted him to feel stupid for having let me go, but I also didn't have any intention of falling back into his arms. I wore casual clothes so it wouldn't be obvious that I had been lounging in pajamas for the last two weeks straight.

I waited for his knock at the door, but when I heard it, I didn't rush to answer. Instead, I kept my palms planted firmly on my kitchen counter and waited for him to knock a second time before I even bothered to start walking over. By the time I opened the door, he was about to knock a third time.

"Hi, Nattie," he grinned and I narrowed my eyes in response. "It's good to see you."

I paused before answering, then said, "You too," then stepped aside, allowing him to come into the house.

"You have a beautiful home," he walked in and looked around.

"Thank you," I said, unsure of how to be a host to my married ex. "Can I get you something to drink?"

"I'd love a beer."

"I have herbal tea, orange juice, and water."

"Actually, some hot tea sounds good," he smiled, putting his hands into the pockets of his tan overcoat, "You're so wholesome now," he added.

"I have health issues," I said as I filled the kettle and put it on the stove.

"Right, I'm sorry," he softly slapped his forehead. "Your mom actually told me all about that. It sounds like you've had a pretty rough year."

"Well, there's a light at the end of the tunnel," I lied. "It can only get better."

"I love your positivity," he said warmly, his eyes attempting to convey some sort of nostalgic adoration that I wasn't in the mood for at all.

"So, how is your wife? I heard you guys had a baby?" I asked, pretending not to know that he had two children; both girls.

"Oh, she's great," he looked down. "When I met her, I was just drawn in by how funny and smart she was."

"That's wonderful. I'm happy for you," I swallowed my bitterness and turned my attention to the whistling kettle.

The latest stoves were more convenient than ever, and it took no time at all to boil water. I poured us each a cup of water and put an herbal tea bag in each one while he talked about his successful financing business and everything he had been up to since he graduated from college. I set his cup at one end of my dining room table and I took my seat at the opposite end. I was growing more and more tired of his company with every passing second and really just wanted him to get his apology out of the way so he could leave.

He sat down and sniffed his tea deeply before setting it aside and attempting to choke out the words he had come to say.

"Natalia, I won't make excuses for how I behaved in high school. I pushed you into the relationship, I manipulated you into bed, I lied and fooled around thinking that it somehow made me powerful to treat others like their feelings didn't matter. But the truth was, I turned into the exact person that I hated most by treating you exactly like my father treated every woman he had ever been with. I won't insult you by telling you I didn't know any better. I knew exactly how much I was hurting you. It wasn't until I became a father that I realized what a shitbag I'd been. I never want my girls to end up with a guy like that."

My jaw almost dropped. I had expected him to come in here with some self-pitying excuse to explain how he was somehow the victim. A genuine heartfelt apology left me so shocked that I wasn't really sure how to respond.

"Thank you," I finally said, shaking off my bewilderment. "I'm glad to see that you've grown up. Your wife must feel really lucky that she met you later in life."

"Yeah, she…" he cleared his throat. "Honestly, she and I don't even sleep in the same bed anymore. After we got married, the focus was on having kids. When we were trying for the girls, we only had sex when she was ovulating, and even then, it wasn't like it was before."

I squirmed in my seat.

*Here we go. I knew he had an angle.*

"I know what you must be thinking," he rubbed the back of his neck. "You're probably figuring that I'm telling you this to make you feel sorry for me. It does seem like something a married guy would say to convince an ex that his marriage is more or less over and that it's okay to fall into bed together."

"Something like that," I said coolly as I sipped my tea.

"I don't blame you," he sniffed the tea again then blew on it. "But the truth is, I just wanted to be honest. I didn't want to walk in here all pretentious about my perfect life when my life is a train wreck except for my job and my kids. I've basically accepted that I'm a glorified sperm donor, and I can't even be angry about it because those girls might be the only thing I've done right."

I smiled as I drew a parallel to my own life. I might not be able to accomplish much from here forward, what with my life being over soon, but I harbored a secret hope that after I died, my son or daughter might spark some sort of positive change, not only for our world but for the universe that lay beyond it.

"I'm happy for you. At least you're there for all your girls' birthdays," I set my cup down. "If my dad had been around, I might have been…" I wasn't sure exactly what words I was searching for. Would I have been more well-rounded, more confident, a happier person? "The truth is, I don't know what I would have been if my dad had been in my life," I finally admitted. "All I know is that I craved his love more than I cared to admit, and being without it broke me in ways that I don't think can ever be healed."

"I know that what I did can't have helped with your pre-existing trust issues. I'm so sincerely sorry, Natalia."

"I forgive you," I said, and as soon as I did, I felt a small weight lift off my shoulders.

Nathan stood and set his cup back down, never having taken a single sip.

"If I could change," he stood up and walked up to me, "maybe he has too."

"That's sweet of you to say," I stood up and put my arms around him. The warmth of his chest and the feeling of his face pressing into my neck was a welcome comfort since it had been a while since I touched anyone. When I let go, his arms lingered around me and his eyes locked with mine as if he was hoping for me to gaze longingly back at him. The familiarity of his closeness woke the long-dormant yearning I'd once had for his love. But I was a grown woman now and not so easily coaxed into abandoning the hard-earned self-respect that I had earned over years of reflection. "I think you should go."

"Of course," he smiled, but his eyes betrayed him. He was never great at hiding his anger. "Thank you for agreeing to meet with me."

I didn't respond but simply nodded with a smile and walked to the door to show him out. After he was gone, I locked the door behind him and sighed. I would have felt better about the whole thing if he had just left it at an apology. If I hadn't hugged him and given him the wrong idea... but no, I wasn't about to take the blame for him being a slime-ball.

I picked out a clean set of pajamas and threw the clothes I was wearing into my hamper. I turned out all the lights then lay in bed and looked at the night sky through my window. Orion's belt twinkled like a familiar friend, lulling me to sleep as I let go and drifted into the darkness.

The sound of something clattering in the kitchen jarred me from my sleep and momentarily eclipsed my despair with alarm. Was that the spoon I had used to dip out the tea bags? Had I set it too close to the edge of the counter and forgotten to put it in the dishwasher? I listened, hearing a second sound I couldn't identify.

Someone was definitely in my house.

I pulled my covers back slowly and tip-toed over to my closet. The closest thing to a weapon I could find was a metal coat hanger. I bent the curved neck into a somewhat straight point. At least I could poke a tiny hole in someone if I had to. I would have to be sure to aim for the eyes or neck if I hoped to do any significant damage.

I peeked out into the hallway. Finding nothing, I crept toward the living room to see a dark silhouette standing by my table, carrying what might have been a box of my things. My anger blinded me to any fear I might have been experiencing. The danger of confronting a burglar paled in comparison to the slow gory death that I was destined to face.

The home invader set the box on the table and turned around. I crouched as I scurried behind the kitchen island, clutching my homemade weapon. If I could shove this firmly into his eyeball or up his nose, I could buy myself enough time to reach the knife block beside the stove. I seized my opportunity and rushed up behind him and jabbed the hanger sharply at his face. The hanger pierced flesh and the robber screamed out in pain.

# Chapter

## ELEVEN

"Lights on, motherfucker!" I yelled. The lights turned on to reveal Korin, wide-eyed and holding me by the wrists.

"It's me," he said, finally letting go and attempting to extract the metal hanger from his cheek. As he pulled it out, a small trickle of bluish-red blood ran down his face before he wiped it off.

"Jesus Christ, Korin," I put my hand on my chest. "Are you trying to give me a heart attack?"

"Your medical records show no indication of heart disease and I have observed your high endurance during cardiovascular activities."

"No," I started to explain, but an uncharacteristic smile spread across his lips. "Are you making a dirty joke?"

I couldn't believe it and simply stared back dumbfounded.

"I have to admit," he straightened his t-shirt, which featured a popular rock band I had introduced him to and that he had clearly grown fond of. "Watching stand-up comedy with you has given me a better understanding of humor."

"Well, you still have a lot to learn," I crossed my arms. "Next time, knock on my front door. What are you doing here, anyway?"

"Allow me to explain," he gestured to the crate that he had set on my table. "It took me a long time to acquire all of the equipment I would need."

"What is all this?" I peeked into the box that was filled with objects I didn't recognize.

"Since you seem resistant to the idea of terminating the pregnancy—"

"What are you? Prophetic? I haven't mentioned shit about it," I snapped, then swiveled around and stormed towards my living room.

It was 02:00 AM. I was supposed to be asleep, not hosting ETs. Especially not ones who would have me as a human lab rat. I slumped heavily on to the couch. I could hear his feet shuffle, while he probably was contemplating an 'appropriate course of action'. I rolled my eyes.

"Well, are you coming?" I eventually forced myself to ask.

"Yes," he replied, and swiftly made his way in and settled a foot behind the couch.

I could feel his gaze on the back of my neck, as though the tip of his finger was lightly tracing down from my hairline. I hated that I loved it.

159

"You gonna sit down or not?" I snapped again. *Really Natalia?*

"Yes," he repeated, and lowered himself on to the cushion beside me then continued to stare.

"Here," I grabbed the TV remote and tapped the chunky green button. "TV. The current stuff. Most of it is shit."

"I see."

He wouldn't take his eyes off me! I tried to concentrate on the colorful seizure-inducing transitions of the lipstick ad, but his presence was extremely difficult to ignore.

"Alright!" I whipped my head in his direction. "What do you want?"

The colors of his eyes seemed a lot more intense here on Earth.

"Seriously, don't you have people to save on your ship? Oh right, I meant kill," I added.

"I..." he searched my eyes and my face. "I notice you are highly distraught."

"You think?"

"I've hurt you. I notice this because you have changed."

I had nothing to say. He was right.

"I have done extensive research on an alternative solution. Mutating the DNA of a primitive lifeform is extremely illegal, but it's relatively simple if you have the right equipment." He began to rush his words. "It must be done in several steps over the course of the next 30 days. If you consent to the procedure, I will have to come here every day to perform an infusion of your cells with Miezen DNA. This hasn't been done in my lifetime, but I am confident I can perform the procedure."

"What? You're kidding right?" I leaned further back on the couch.

"There is no risk to the fetus… if that is what you've decided on that matter," he continued, then paused as if he expected an answer. "If it works, you could live on my planet. If the procedure fails, or your cells reject the infusion, you will not be in a worse position than the one you're in right now."

"Okay, enough. Please just go now."

Wide-eyed, Korin looked at his hands which were resting on his legs. He slowly stood up and walked back to the table to pick up his crate and disappeared before my eyes, leaving a subtle glow on the ceiling directly above where he had been standing.

I went back to bed and closed my eyes, trying not to think about the things that he had just said. I fell asleep sooner than I expected.

When I woke up, I looked in the mirror and realized that I didn't recognize this shell of a woman staring back at me. I took a long, steamy shower, shaved my legs, and washed my hair. After I got out, I fired up my blow-dryer - it had been in a drawer ever since I decided to check out of my life.

I knew that if I called Laura I would only get yelled at, so I decided against it. I spent a few hours researching the current wedding trends. I even designed a concept board outlining the process used by professional wedding planners to select venues, flowers, appetizers, and meals, etc. After it was done, I worked up the courage to call Abiola. She had always been a little bit more understanding when I dropped off the grid.

"Natalia?" Abiola sounded surprised that I was calling and reasonably so.

"Yeah, it's me," I said, hoping that the smile I had forced on to my face was coming through in my voice. "I'm sorry I've been out of touch. I was thinking, we could all get together in the next week or two. I made an action plan for planning weddings. Maybe we could..."

"Actually, we already made most of the big decisions already. We're just down to seating arrangements and boring stuff like that."

"I.. I love boring stuff," I stammered. "Do you want to go out for coffee? You can give me the details and I'll get it done for you."

"That's okay, sweetie," Abiola's maternal tone was meant to be soothing, but it cut me like a knife. "We have the wedding stuff pretty well in hand, but we could still go out sometime. Have you talked to Laura?"

"No, I've been so tired, I hardly get out of bed and I know she probably hates me for not returning her calls."

"Girl, don't even give me that self-pity BS," Abiola tried to sound stern. "You could have picked up a phone and just told her you weren't feeling good. The more time that goes by, the more hurt her feelings are going to be."

"You're right," I closed my eyes.

"How 'bout this Friday night, but you call Laura and make plans to go out before then, just the two of you. You have to talk to her. You know how much she worries about you."

"I know. But let me get back to you about Friday. It's hard to say how I'll be feeling on any given day."

"Okay," Abiola agreed. "We'll play it by ear."

"Sounds good. Bye Abi."

"Later, sweetie."

Getting off the phone, I realized that I hadn't been corresponding with my boss at all. He would probably want to know what happened to my work tablet and if or when I was planning to come back to work. I used my phone to check my bank account. All my bills were set to pay out automatically and I had enough savings to live off of for a year if I wanted to. Seeing a large deposit from work, I couldn't help but suspect that I had been terminated and paid out for all my vacation time.

I got dressed and did my hair and makeup. Maybe if I went down there in person, I could beg for another chance. As I opened my front door, I was surprised to see Korin standing there with his crate of space gadgets.

"What are you doing here?"

"Time is running out to decide what to do about…"

"Shh!" I scowled, pulling him inside as I waved at my neighbor who was in his front yard staring at Korin.

He set down his crate again.

"Knowledge is the enemy of fear," he announced. "The more you are educated about your situation and the options at your disposal to handle said situation, the less fearful you will be."

"The option you're referring to is getting my DNA altered and leaving my life behind to live with you on an alien planet."

"Yes, it's a relatively simple procedure with minimal risk to you and the fetus."

"Then why is it so illegal? I've seen the lengths that your people are willing to go to."

"My society views humanity as a lower form of life. To them, it would be like putting the mind of a dog into the body of a human being."

"Huh," I frowned at the thought of a grown man trying to sniff another man's butt.

"I can teach you our customs," Korin's eyes were aflame with excitement. "I have created an identity for you. We can marry and raise this child as our own, far away from this place. I will work as a doctor in my homeworld and you can learn all about the universe beyond your own solar system." He said, sounding ever so slightly breathless at the idea of it as he described this new life to me. His fingertips lifted my chin so that I would meet his gaze. "I would take care of you."

I shook off the gesture and backed away.

"If I go with you, how do you know it's because I care for you and not because I don't want to die?" I challenged.

"I wouldn't force you to do anything you don't want to do. However, if I change you into one of us, it is unlikely that you will be able to hide what you are for long. Staying here would put you at risk because your appearance will be altered. Going to my homeworld would be dangerous because you don't know our ways. Without me to guide you, on my world you would likely become a vagrant, and on your world, you would likely become a figurative guinea pig. If you would at least pretend to be my mate, your chance of survival and quality of life

165

would improve drastically. There is also the matter of the child."

He was trying to save my life, but I couldn't help hesitating.

"I understand the situation," I swallowed hard. "But this is a big decision and it's my life, so I'm going to need a day or two to think things over."

"I can give you 72 hours. But after that, we risk not being able to complete the procedure in time."

"Thank you," I nodded. "So... where did you get those clothes?"

"I bartered for them at a retail store in exchange for American currency. I will return every 24 hours to check in and see if you have made your final decision," he said, then picked up his crate and walked into my guest bedroom. "Remember that the opportunity will not be available forever so do not take too long to make a decision."

By the time I made it through the doorway, he had vanished and the crate was sitting on the dresser. Now that I had seen him again, there was no question in my mind about whether or not I cared for Korin. I had allowed myself to drop my defenses. I never would have for anyone else. However, I also knew for a fact that his culture was literally lightyears away from what I was used to. Did I really want to commit to a life lived among people who could never know the truth about who I was?

I sat down at my computer and looked at the empty search bar. I had spent so much time hiding from the situation, it was probably too late to let Korin terminate the pregnancy... safely anyway. I typed in alternate methods for terminating a pregnancy. Several articles recommended different combinations of medications and herbs that force a miscarriage. I knew even as I looked over all the options that this was not a normal pregnancy and that none of these methods would have a high chance of working, given my unique circumstances. My eyes clouded with tears. I never thought I'd be the type of person that would be looking up DIY abortion sites. But at least it wasn't some careless decision that got me to this point, I told myself. This was forced on me.

I had spent my entire adult life being responsible and always trying to do the right thing. I felt a stab of guilt for all the times I looked down on women for deciding not to keep a baby they were responsible for creating. I felt so ashamed, imagining how many of those women were making those decisions to save their lives, sometimes in a literal sense and sometimes simply to preserve the life that they've spent years building for themselves.

Before Korin came along, I had loved my job. I had spent every waking moment since high school working toward becoming the person I had become. Now, here I was on the cusp of accomplishing everything I had ever set out to do and, one way or another, it was all about to be over. No matter how this played out, I was either going to die drowning in my own blood like that poor woman I saw on the ship or be forced into being Korin's pretend wife for the rest of my life.

I didn't even know how women were treated on his planet. What if wives are supposed to be subservient to their male counterparts? I would have to learn about religion, war, history, and planets that I had never even heard of. What was I supposed to do with all the wasted years of education on Earth?

Not to mention, I had a deep love of the arts, and that was something that was not merely unappreciated by his culture but frowned upon. There would be no more movies to watch, no more novels to read, no songs to listen to, and absolutely no paintings to admire. Painting - the thing I loved most in all the world - would be something that could be dangerous if someone found out I was doing it.

Would a life without art really be worth living? Art was always humanity's greatest unifying force, in my opinion. To me, it had always defined what it meant to be human. This felt like a deeper truth than before, now that a so-called superior race of beings had no understanding or appreciation of it. I may not have ever been someone who had a healthy relationship with my emotions, but I had learned to embrace them as part of my humanity. This, my humanity, was something that I appreciated now more than ever before, now that I faced the choice of dying or losing it forever.

What if there was an afterlife? What if becoming Miezen took away my ability to feel, and in turn, caused me to forfeit my immortal soul? Was it worth it? I put my hand on my belly. Inside of me was a person who would grow up with half of my DNA. What if he or she loves art, but has no one to explain what it is and why it's important.

I walked into my bedroom and looked at my reflection in the mirror on my closet door. Lifting my shirt, I stared at myself wondering where the little creature was positioned in there. By simply being a good mother, I could alter the course of history and save who-knows-how-many women from the breeding program. If I could become educated enough and gain social status, maybe I could become an advocate for humans under the guise of a Miezen woman.

There were a lot of maybes and it was a long sleepless night. The sun came up and I spent the day reading a new novel I had started, savoring every paragraph, knowing that no matter what I decided, I would soon pick up the last book I would ever read.

A knock on the door made me jump.

"Korin?" I walked to the door and opened it without even bothering to look through the peephole. I felt my expression change when I saw that it was Nathan standing on my doorstep.

"Hi," he took a drag off his cigarette and I covered my mouth. The smell of smoke made me feel instantly nauseated. "Sorry, I forgot," he put out his cigarette in my decorative gravel and left the butt there before inviting himself in.

"What do you want, Nathan?"

"I want you to slap me in the face and tell me I'm an asshole."

"What?" My face scrunched up. "Uh… why?"

"Because of how I acted," he took his fedora off and hung his head. "I misread the situation and I can't stop feeling horrible about it. I really just came here with the intention of being your friend and I fucked it up."

"You didn't fuck it up," I huffed, rolling my eyes. "I'm just not interested in getting involved with a married man."

"That's because you're a decent human being; something I'm still working on these days."

"Decent might be a stretch but I'm trying," I replied. I felt uncomfortable when people tried to make me out to be a saint when I spent so much time and energy resenting everyone.

"I'd like a chance to start over. How about I bring you some dinner tomorrow? Just as a friend," he said and put his hands up defensively.

"My diet is really specific."

"Come on, you can cheat just once, can't you? I know this place downtown that makes the most amazing steak you've ever had."

"I once ate a tortilla chip without thinking about it and I ended up hospitalized for four days."

"Okay, no dinner," he crossed his arms. "What about a movie? It can be one of those space-alien action flicks you used to love so much."

"You remember that?" I blushed in spite of myself.

"Hell yes, I do!" Nathan laughed. "Remember you went to that Halloween party as the space captain of that show we used to watch?"

"That was a great party," I nodded, recalling the blur of colorful pool-toys, beer pong, and rooftop karaoke.

"I'm surprised you remember any of it! You were pretty drunk," Nathan said teasingly with a chuckle.

"Yeah, those were good times."

"They meant more to me than I realized at the time," he scratched his chin. "You were a lot of fun."

"Once upon a time," I shrugged.

"Alright," he walked toward the door. "I won't keep you up anymore, but tomorrow night, friends only movie date. You could even invite a few friends if you want. Text me what you can eat, and I'll bring some snacks."

"Fine," I responded without thinking.

*What the hell?*

I definitely do not want to cozy up on the couch with my married ex to watch a movie and chill. But it was too late to take it back now. I would have to text him while he was at work and cancel. Then I would just refuse to respond to his calls or texts from then on.

Before I could get back to my bedroom, I spotted Nathan's hat still sitting on my entrance table. I picked it up just as there was a knock on the door again.

"Forget something?" I asked as I opened the door. Korin stood awkwardly on my doorstep clutching a chrome briefcase and sporting an insecure-looking frown.

"No, I just did not want to scare you again by appearing inside."

I pulled him inside hurriedly.

"What if someone sees you?"

"But you told me to use the front…"

"I know what I said," I snapped. "Now that I've had time to think about it, I agree with your original method of randomly appearing somewhere in my house. Just try to announce your presence before I attack your face."

"Human females are confusing," he shook his head. "But also interesting."

"Thanks?"

"Have you decided how you wish to proceed?"

"No," I sighed. "I haven't. I never realized what a privilege it is to be human and have all these emotions at my disposal. I'm not sure that a life without my human emotions is one that I want to live."

"I feel emotions," Korin put his hand on my shoulder. "I would not wish to take away the things that make you who you are. The Miezen way is to consciously learn to suppress our emotions. They believe that acting on them without considering the facts is reckless and destructive behavior. However, it was my emotions that spurred me to try and save you and, so far, I do not have any regrets."

"Oh really?" I raised an inquisitive eyebrow. "And why is that?"

He set his briefcase down on the counter.

"You have taught me a lot since our first interaction," he said and clasped one hand around the other as if to

173

soothe himself. "I have learned about the value of intuition, music, art, and novels, as well as many other things. We learn about human values from a distance at the academy, but to have a human explain it in a way I can understand has proved to be an enlightening experience."

"That's a pretty good answer," I had to admit, he was too sweet to be a sociopath, no matter what his culture found acceptable, but I still wasn't ready to give up my identity.

"There is no word for *love* in the Miezen language," Korin shifted his weight and looked down at his folded hands as he spoke. "My brother was the person I held in the highest esteem as a child. More so than my mother or father. He helped me, not by simply going over the facts of my lessons with me, but by assuring me that I was capable and worthy of the work I wanted to do. I wanted to live up to the potential he saw in me when my parents only saw the qualities I lacked."

"You wanted to make him proud."

"Yes," his eyes widened as he relaxed, knowing that I understood what he was trying to say. "When he was injured in the field, his physicians knew that he would not recover. I wished to travel to where he was so that I could tell him how much his encouragement had meant to me. I wanted to be with him when he took his final breaths and perhaps assure him that he had contributed to the universe in a meaningful way."

"It's only natural to want to say goodbye to someone you love."

"Well, my parents were more concerned with me falling behind in my studies again. I was not permitted to see my brother as he lay dying in the medical bay of some ship orbiting Earth, lightyears from the academy."

"I'm so sorry, Korin."

"It was pointless to think about at the time. The practical way to honor my brother would have been to study harder and excel in my academic endeavors. But I was deeply distressed and unable to focus. I barely passed my final exams and my parents continued being embarrassed by my continuous underachievement. Even with my obvious disability, I managed to secure a high-ranking position in the medical field. I was placed on the breeding ship but my professors knew I wanted to work in the field. They wanted me to prove that my emotions wouldn't affect my ability to do my job. I have failed."

"I know that your culture values intellect," I put my hand on his cheek. "But our emotions are not a disease that needs to be cured. Our intellect is only half of who we are, emotions can help us to see things our logical minds would otherwise miss."

"You are referring to intuition," he furrowed his brow. "Data that is processed by the subconscious and cannot be consciously quantified."

"I guess so," I shrugged.

"What is your intuition telling you now?"

I still felt unsure, but the reckless abandon that had brought us together felt like something I needed to trust. I took a deep breath and held it before blurting out the words.

"Let's do it," I blurted out. Yup, I was going to turn myself into a blue species and have a cute baby alien. My hand instinctively traveled to my abdomen. I allowed myself to smile, just a little.

He put his hand over his heart.

"Your decision makes me feel very happy and relieved," Korin exhaled. "May I kiss you?"

"No," I took a step back, not entirely sure I had fully forgiven him.

"Alright," he said, then folded his hands and looked down. "I will need a room where I can set up all of my equipment where it will not be seen or touched by anyone besides the two of us."

"Let's use my guest bedroom since the crate is already in there. Will I need a chair or a bed?"

"A bed would be the safest. If the infusion occurs too quickly, your body may go into convulsions. I will have to construct an airtight chamber that will contain your entire body during each session."

"Great," I said. I shook my head and led him to my guest room where he started assembling his portable laboratory.

"I am learning to appreciate sarcasm," he said as he took out various objects and arranged them on the dresser. "You were being sarcastic."

I was beginning to realize that, whatever my future held, Korin would look out for me, even if we weren't together. However strange and alien he seemed, he was more human than he realized. After all, he was risking everything to save the life of a creature he was taught was an inferior life form. Some might believe that chivalry and selflessness were uniquely human attributes. But after everything I was going through, I knew better.

Korin took several tiles of what looked like thick durable glass. The tiles were about six-inch squares, but they fit together seamlessly as he used them to form a large glass coffin that sat on the bed. Opening the chrome case that he had brought with him, a machine unfolded revealing a cylindrical object.

"What's this?"

"It's a pump," he said, not bothering to look up. "It will cycle your blood in a similar way a dialysis machine does." Unrolling several coils of tubing, he continued,

"Your blood will pass through the machine beneath the pump and alter your blood cells."

"I see," I swallowed, feeling the chill of uncertainty creeping back in.

"To prevent your body from rejecting your new Miezen blood, we are going to use these lights to infuse your skin cells," he held up a spherical light that was about the size of a softball. "The longer we can keep you under these lights, the better chance you have of making the transition without complication. You should probably urinate, eat, and do anything you can to ensure you won't need to leave this chamber for a minimum of eighteen hours."

"Sounds like fun," I frowned, looking down at the glass coffin. Eighteen hours was a long time.

"You are being sarcastic again," Korin said with a small grin.

# Chapter
## TWELVE

After using the restroom and eating as big of a meal as I could manage, I stood in the doorway of the guest room for a moment and just watched Korin work. I hadn't forgiven him altogether, not after everything I had been through, but I was nervous and it took a conscious effort not to ask him a million questions about what he'd been up to since I left the ship.

"I guess we should get started," I ran my fingers over the transparent enclosure to find that the glass was surprisingly warm.

"Since you are reaching the final stages of pregnancy, the chances of the procedure being successful are optimal if we begin immediately."

I realized that my only chance was to stop swimming against the current and move forward. After all, the future was barreling towards me whether I chose to accept it or not.

"And I'm supposed to get naked inside this thing?"

"Yes," Korin replied in a matter of fact way. He began hooking up cylindrical pumps and attaching the tubing that would be filtering my blood, infusing it, and returning it to my body. "There is no need to feel embarrassed. I have seen your body many times over the last year."

I knew he was right, and it seemed pointless to ask him to step out when he was going to spend the next 18 hours observing me as I lay in this thing. He was facing away while fiddling with the settings on the cylinder that was sitting on my dresser.

"I guess you're right," I said, setting my phone down on the nightstand.

I pulled my shirt off over my head, grateful that I had just spent the morning grooming myself after having neglected shaving for the last couple of weeks. I slipped off my smart-band and placed it on the dresser. He didn't look at me but did speak after a few seconds.

"Do you need help getting into the chamber?"

"How do you open it?" I asked.

"Find the seam at the upper left-hand corner. That is the weakest point in the seal."

I did as he instructed, and the lid peeled free of the rubbery seal that held it on. I leaned against the wall and found that the glass panel was incredibly light. Cautiously, I climbed in and lay down.

"Okay, now what?"

"I'm going to seal you inside," he said, turning to me.

His eyes didn't linger on my skin and I felt myself relax. I appreciated the fact that he was rather good at keeping things clinical. He picked up a mechanism that was about the size of an old-fashioned smoke detector and used some sort of fast-acting adhesive to stick it to the right side by my head. On my left, he did the same with the pump and arranged the tubes before cleaning a spot on my forearm. He inserted one needle for the blood coming out and another for the blood to go back in less than an inch away from the first one.

He put the lid back in place and the seal seemed to cause a suction.

"Will I be able to breathe in here?" I asked, feeling a sudden panic welling up in my chest.

"Don't worry," Korin's voice came through the speaker. "The same device that is allowing us to communicate is also slowly converting the carbon dioxide you are inhaling into breathable oxygen. This is rather old technology used by Miezen explorers on space and deep-sea expeditions."

"Well, I guess you learn something new every day," I muttered. I looked to my right at the little device. "I hope it works. How old did you say it was?"

"I made sure all this equipment was functional before bringing it here," he said, however, he kept his gaze on the object in his hands; it looked like a tablet. "I'll be continuously monitoring your vitals. You don't need to worry, I will not let any harm come to you or your baby."

I felt a twinge of self-consciousness pass through me as I put my hand on my abdomen. I had never thought of myself as mother material. My thoughts drifted back to my poor dead goldfish, floating belly-up over his little castle. I swallowed, hoping that I was ready for all the unexpected things that awaited me.

"Will the baby be really small? Like... a lot smaller than a human baby?"

He placed small lights on top of the glass enclosure and turned them on. It was pleasantly warm, and it reminded me of that one time Laura made me go with her to a tanning booth.

"At birth, most Miezen babies weigh about three pounds. Once exposed to the proper atmosphere, they grow fairly quickly, gaining about one pound per day over the first ten days. After that, their development slows and is more similar to that of a human child."

"That's a pretty efficient way to have a baby. No need to get all huge and uncomfortable. No stretch marks."

"Miezen people are anatomically superior in many ways. You'll find yourself feeling much healthier, it will be easier to learn new things, and our ability to send images along with spoken word makes communication much more efficient."

"Can you do it across great distances?"

"I wish that were possible, but no. It has a limited range. The greater your bond with the subject you're trying to communicate with, the further the range."

Over the next several hours, Korin talked to me about his planet's history, the various cultures, and the flora and fauna that populated it. After a while, I started dozing off and found myself immersed in a vividly colorful dream. I was walking through a beautifully lush jungle where I found a small fern-like plant that was constantly changing color. I looked closer to see a small four-legged insect beside it that had a pretty blue shell.

The sound of my doorbell woke me up and Korin was standing over me, holding my phone against the glass. I could see my illuminated screen where Nathan was texting me telling me he was going to call an ambulance if I didn't answer.

"Text him and tell him I'm okay!" I barked at Korin.

"This is inefficient," he complained as he slowly pushed each key.

"Try pushing the speech to text icon - the microphone icon - and just speak into the phone!"

I heard my phone beep as it went into speech to text mode.

"Natalia is unharmed. Please leave," he spoke flatly.

"No!" I tried to sit up and hit my head on the glass. "Do not send that!" I said. "Pretend to be me and say,

'Sorry, I was asleep. I don't feel up to hanging out today. Raincheck question mark'."

Korin repeated what I said and then showed me the screen. I looked and made sure he deleted the previous statement and told him to send it.

Nathan responded.

*Are you serious? Maybe next time give me a little more notice if you're going to flake out on me.*

I clenched my jaw, wishing I could run up to the door and tell him off for being a douchebag. Alright, so I had made plans with him that I had no intention of following through with. On top of it, I'd forgotten to cancel, which was my only real mistake. But he had a wife at home and didn't need to be trying to weasel his way into my life.

I would need to remember to call Abiola and cancel my plans with her. She had tasked me with calling Laura and at least trying to apologize, which I wasn't quite ready to do yet. As for my job, it didn't look like I was going to need it anyway. Now that I had started this transformation, there was little point in turning back now.

After Nathan left, Korin and I both let out a sigh of relief.

He smiled and said, "That could have been very awkward and difficult to explain if an ambulance arrived to take you to the hospital."

"Yes, it would have," I groaned into my hands. "How many sessions will this take?"

"It depends on how easily your body accepts the infusion. At first, it may try to correct the changes, but the more persistent we are, the faster your body will adjust and accept its new state."

We still had seven more hours to kill and I was horribly bored. The communication device didn't allow me to hear music very well. Even if I had him turn it up uncomfortably loud (for Korin), I could barely hear it. Korin said that the com-device was designed to focus on and enhance the voice of the person wearing it. He took it out of his ear to show me; it reminded me of a single wireless earbud. He set up my tablet next to the bed and I watched a movie without the luxury of sound. It didn't matter much though. It was a movie I had watched many times as a kid, so I could have recited it word for word if I had to.

I managed to convince him to read me the novel I had started. He sounded so awkward and uncomfortable but it made me feel a little giddy inside to see him squirming through reading a romance novel in an attempt to keep me entertained and at ease.

It was six in the morning by the time we were done. He pulled the lid off and I felt a hiss as the cool air from my house delighted my skin. I had begun sweating only slightly after being under the lights for a full day. I was actually surprised that I didn't feel hotter than I was. I thought for sure I'd at least have a sunburn, but my skin felt fine. The worst thing was how stiff I felt after having lain flat on my back for so long.

Korin helped me get out and I went to shower. When I got out, I found that he had brought me some food he had prepared back on the ship. We sat on the couch and ate together as we chatted about the book and what we thought might happen next.

"I would not have read fiction, if not for this experience. It has been a fascinating experience."

"Glad I could help you further broaden your horizons," I said, my tone sarcastic, but I wasn't as irritated as I sounded.

"Do you expect anyone else might come to visit during our sessions?"

"I hope not," I answered. "I have a pretty non-existent social life, but my mom worries about me and my friends..." I shook my head and looked away.

"What about your coworkers?"

"I've basically given up on my job. I thought it meant everything to me, but given what's happened, it wasn't really as important as I thought it was."

"I don't believe you really feel that way."

"I guess you're right," I swallowed my bitterness. "I worked really hard to get where I was and I'm angry and sad that it was all for nothing. But I can handle it. The thing that hurts most is losing Laura and Abiola. Don't even get started on my mom. Not just because I'm leaving, but up until this point, I've really messed things up with them. I make plans and don't follow through with them. They have important life changes that they're going through, and I've been completely wrapped up in my own depression."

"You have been going through big life changes too," Korin said, locking his eyes on mine. "You just haven't been able to talk about yours."

"What do your people do for recreational activities?" I changed the subject.

"Different individuals enjoy different things."

"Are there competitive sports on Miez?"

"No," he smiled. "I have observed a recorded game of American football. It seems an odd thing to risk such serious injuries over."

"I sort of agree with you," I nodded. "So, your recreational activities are limited to what; hiking and swimming?"

"We also interact with plants and animals."

"You keep pets?"

"We keep plants for food." His expression grew thoughtful. "Animals belong in their natural habitats. All of the animals on Miez are herbivores. There are some forms of carnivorous plants. We have tried to eradicate them, but they always seem to pop up in remote areas."

"So, the wild animals are all friendly?"

"Mostly, yes," he nodded and took a bite of his food. "For thousands of years, they have had nothing to fear. Since there are no predators, there is no need for them to be afraid."

"That's kind of amazing, I can't even imagine a natural world with no predators."

"You will love to look at all the colors there. There are many beautiful things I wish to show you."

A picture started to form in my mind of the fern with the blue bug on it, but it faded before I could imagine it clearly. I decided to show Korin how to do yoga, which he took to very well. His balance was excellent, and he was obviously very strong. Even though he started out looking stiff and awkward, he got the hang of it quickly.

After taking a day to rest, I moved around as much as I could before beginning another infusion session. Once it was complete, Korin explained that he had something he needed to take care of on his ship. He said that he would be gone for a few days. During his absence, I bit the bullet and finally met Abiola for lunch.

I got there early and was already seated at a table on the patio when she showed up. She looked surprised and actually smiled when she saw me, which made me feel less terrified about our upcoming interaction. Holding her arms out, she shuffled past the other tables and I stood up to hug her.

"You showed up," she smiled.

"I did," I replied sheepishly.

"Well, I'm happy to see you," she said, then raised an eyebrow quizzically. "Did you call Laura yet?"

I didn't answer but looked away.

"That girl does her damnedest to look out for you. She deserves a best friend that returns her phone calls."

"I know," I whispered. "I feel like I've fucked up so bad that there's no way to save it at this point."

"That's a coward's excuse, and you know it."

"Yeah. You're right."

When we sat down to eat, we didn't talk about the wedding, or work, or my illness. It felt like neither of us wanted to touch on those subjects.

Most of our lunch was spent in silence. Halfway through the meal, Abiola got a nostalgic smile on her face as she looked at the water in her glass.

"Remember the time you spilled your drink on the guy at the pool?"

"Oh my gosh!" I leaned back and thought about it. "I was so drunk."

"He gave you his number though. Whatever happened with that?"

"I probably lost it or threw it away."

"What?"

"That's a horrible way to meet someone. I can't tell my kids that I met their father at a pool party. I think I ended up throwing up in the shrubs at some point."

She laughed and everything got quiet again. The only things we really had to talk about were things we did a long time ago. It was at that point that I realized there were no new memories to be made and that this was probably the last time that I was ever going to see her. I studied the little details, things that I would remember years from then. The bracelet she was wearing had been a birthday present from me three years prior. Lines that were starting to form around her eyes from smiling with all her heart.

I could tell she wanted to push me towards speaking to Laura again. The last time I saw Laura was that day in the elevator and that didn't sit well with me. But at the same time, it's not like my friends were going to be able to throw me a going away party.

"It's been good seeing you, Nat," Abiola said later as we hugged goodbye. "You take care of yourself and, for the love of god, pick up the phone once in a while."

"I'll try," I squeaked, but the lump in my throat made it hard to speak. "Bye, Abi."

I tried to say goodbye as if I planned on seeing her again, but I knew this would be the last time. She smiled and turned to walk away and I stood there trying to detach from my feelings before making my own way home. No one said it would be easy and I knew the hardest part would be letting go.

My phone rang - it was Nathan. I swiped and sent him to voicemail. I was done with him. When I did text him, it was always short and to the point. As much as I enjoyed talking to him that one time that he had been over, I didn't need that kind of drama in my life at this point.

The way he behaved on the day after my third session really drove home what a manipulative douche bag he was. I figured it was him when the doorbell went off and he started knocking immediately after. I picked up my phone to text him to tell him to leave, but I saw several missed calls and texts from both him and my mother. I opened my texts and sure enough... they were both coming over to *check on me*. My worst nightmare was coming true. I went to the door in my robe and answered.

"What the hell is wrong with you that you can't answer your damn..." My mother stopped bitching and gasped. "Oh my god. Nattie, what's wrong with you?"

"What are you talking about?" I scowled. "You can't just barge in on me and expect me to be ready to entertain company!"

"Sweetheart, you're blue!" Her eyes grew wide as she reached out to touch my face.

"Oh that," I said dodging her hand. "It's makeup, I'm practicing for a costume contest that's coming up," I replied, trying to conceal my surprise. I had been looking in the mirror every single day, looking for signs that the procedures were working. I hadn't noticed any changes in my skin tone, but I hadn't looked at my reflection in direct sunlight either.

"Jesus, Nattie," she frowned. "You're obviously having some sort of mental breakdown."

"No, Mom," I rolled my eyes. "What's actually happening is that you're bringing my high-school boyfriend who has a fucking wife and kids to my house to check on me for no reason. If anyone is mental, it's you. Nathan has an excuse because he's a narcissistic cheating asshole and he can't help himself," I snapped, gesturing toward Nathan who feigned an offended expression before looking down. "You, on the other hand, are supposed to be a well-balanced functional adult with a grown child who has left the nest," I continued. She began interrupting me, but I lashed out further, raising my voice so that I almost yelled, "You just can't stand the thought that now that I'm a grown woman, we have nothing in common. So, excuse me if I avoid your phone calls."

"You could at least text me and let me know you're alright," she retorted curtly and reached forward to try and push past me to come inside.

"Um, no," I said, then put my hand on her shoulder and barred her from walking in. "That's not happening. You need an invitation before you just walk into my house."

I knew full well that I was being a huge asshole, but I couldn't risk letting them in and being distracted with one of them while the other snooped through my home. If they saw the set up in my guest room, there would be too much to explain.

"What has gotten into you? It's not drugs?" She asked, squinting at me. "Is it?"

"No, Mom," I said, and jabbed my forefinger at her. "I don't need a goddamn intervention from you two. I'm physically sick. If I tried to put drugs in my body, I'd probably be in the hospital or dead. Did it ever cross your mind that I'm tired of you calling to remind me of how pathetic my life is? Maybe I'm done talking to you about my ever-waning social life and the fact that I'm never going to get married. Maybe I've come to accept my life exactly as it is, and I don't need you trying to push your expectations of a socially acceptable life down my throat."

"I didn't realize you felt that way. You never talk to me about what you're feeling."

"Well, I'm telling you now," I said firmly, then looked at Nathan. "So, it would be great if you could just go home and pay attention to your wife." Turning back to my mom, I continued, "And you can just take a page out of Dad's book and call me every year on my birthday."

I slammed the door, heart racing and hating myself. I know I could have handled that better. But in my defense, I had never had my mother and my ex show up on my doorstep unexpectedly at the same time. And I might have reacted differently if I wasn't in full-blown panic mode.

I looked down at my trembling hands and took a few deep breaths. *It's going to be okay*, I told myself. Korin would be back in an hour or two, and soon after that, we would both be far away from all of this. My stomach tied itself into a knot. I couldn't let that be the last interaction I had with my mother. I knew that, no matter what, I would need to make sure everything was okay between us before I left for good.

After an hour or so, Nathan texted me that he was sorry for dropping in on me. He told me it was my mom's idea, which was probably true. I texted back *'it's fine'* and hoped that he would just leave me alone. I didn't want to see him anymore, to fight or make up or for any other reason. I just needed him to leave me alone. I walked over to my sofa and curled up into the fetal position.

"Natalia," Korin's voice came from my guest room. "I am here."

He walked out into the living room carrying a small potted plant that had several pods on it.

"I just had to run my mother and Nathan off my doorstep," I told him, my voice still shaking from the memory of it.

"Your former lover?"

"That would be the one."

"Oh," he said distantly, as though unsure of why I was sharing that information with him. "I have brought you something I thought you might like."

"New fruit to try?" I asked

"This one is not good for eating, although you can if you fall on hard times," he set it on my coffee table before sitting at the opposite end of the couch. I noticed that its small branches and leaves were constantly moving although it was very subtle. The pods seemed to roll around in a circle, almost like a swiveling eyeball looking around the room. "Feel one of the pods," Korin instructed and gestured toward the plant with a slight smile.

I reached out and touched the pod, which squeaked as it shriveled up and transformed into a tiny raisin-like ball.

"Oh! What the hell is that?" I jerked my hand back.

"It won't hurt you," he said. "Miezen children often have one in their bedrooms. It is a good first plant for a child to have. It helps them to learn how to care for other more complex plants. It is a basic life skill on Miez. Children also like them because they make amusing noises."

Korin touched another pod and it sounded as if it blew a raspberry as it shriveled up.

"That's so funny," I touched another pod and it made a whistling sound.

"How does it make so many different noises?"

"Its larger cousin is the carnivorous plant I mentioned before," he answered. "It mimics simple noises that it hears. The bigger ones can mimic animals and even Miezen voices if they live long enough to learn. The larger variety is dangerous and far less amusing."

"I bet," I said, smiling and reaching to touch another pod.

"Are you ready to start another session?" he asked.

"I suppose so," I sighed and stood up.

"I can see that you're beginning to exhibit the physical characteristics of my species."

"Oh," I blinked. "My mother mentioned that I looked blue."

I walked off to the bathroom and turned the lights on. To my surprise, I was starting to look different. My bone structure was more stoic and there was a distinct blue sheen to my skin. I wasn't sure, but I also felt an inch or two taller. I met Korin in the guest room where he was already turning on all the equipment. I shed my bathrobe just as he turned around and, for the first time since we had begun these procedures, he looked me up and down.

"Your body seems to be adjusting to the infusions even faster than I predicted. Two or three more sessions should be all that is needed."

"What do you think?" I said holding my hands out to the side.

"I am pleased that your body isn't rejecting the infusion. In fact, I do not think it will take nearly as long as I originally expected," he said with an approving nod.

He took the lid off the infusion chamber and helped me get settled in. I couldn't help wondering whether he was still attracted to me now that I looked different. He seemed to be in doctor-mode, which was exactly what I had wanted when we started these sessions. But the more time we spent together, the more I wondered what it would be like to be married to him. Did I really plan on marrying him only to be his platonic roommate?

During the session, I slept on and off and Korin employed our usual strategies for keeping me entertained. When it was over, Korin helped me get out and I got directly into the shower. When I got out, Korin had fallen asleep in the armchair in my guest room.

"Korin," I touched his arm.

"I am sorry," he said. "I will go back to the E-Orbiter-3 and come back tomorrow."

"Actually," I swallowed, "you can sleep here if you want. We're going to be living together soon. We may as well get used to it."

"I will sleep here tonight if you wish," he said. "I will have to return to the ship to work tomorrow. I have been choosing to forego sleep in order to observe you during your sessions. Even without sleep, I have had to shift my schedule around multiple times. My superiors will notice that the quality of my work is compromised if I do not sleep soon. They will assume I am having a medical issue and detain me if I am not careful."

"You've been going without sleep to take care of me?"

"Now that I know your body is accepting the infusion, I will be able to sleep during your session if I am tired. Miezens only sleep for about four hours in a 24 hour period. We can go up to a week without sleep before it begins to affect our health and job performance."

"Well, let's go get some rest," I said and nodded toward the doorway.

He followed me to my bedroom and seemed to pass out immediately after laying down on top of the blankets. I grabbed a throw from my couch and put it over him before unbuckling his boots and pulling them off. He was so exhausted that he barely stirred, turning over on his side to face the middle of the bed.

I climbed under the blankets on the other side and looked at him for a few seconds before closing my eyes. The sound of his breathing was a gentle reminder that I wasn't going to be alone after this. What his people were doing to mine was unforgivable. But on the other hand, he didn't choose this job. Much like the countless people who have joined the military in many countries throughout Earth's history; people are sometimes called to carry out a duty that they don't agree with. It didn't mean that they were bad people.

Korin was risking everything to save me. He was forced into this line of work; he didn't choose it. And after being placed here by whatever powers that be, he went against what was in his own best interest in favor of doing what he felt was right. How long did I really plan on punishing him for things he had no control over?

I reached over and touched the back of my fingers to his cheek. In spite of his clinical nature, he possessed a tenderness that I didn't fully understand. I drifted off to sleep and, upon waking, saw that he had gone. I jumped up and rushed to peek into the guest room. He wasn't there, but the sound of movement in the kitchen made me sigh with relief.

He was cutting fruit and placing the slices on a plate.

"That looks good," I said as I opened a cupboard and took out a jar of almonds. I put a handful of almonds on the plate and he looked at me with a shy smile before looking away.

"It's for both of us," he set the plate on the table.

"Is it common for your people to share a plate?" I asked, following him to the dining room table.

"Only if there is a level of trust and esteem shared," he sat down. "It's similar to sharing a bed."

I sat across from him and we each took turns picking slices of fruit off the plate.

"After the last session," Korin's face grew serious, "we must go back to the breeding ship." Reading the change in my posture, he tried to assure me. "I won't let anything happen to you. You will look just like one of us and no one will question your presence there. The final procedure will take place in my quarters on the E-Orbiter-3. It will be a crucial step in the process. If it doesn't work, all this will have been for nothing. It will allow you to understand and speak Miezen as easily as you speak English."

"Then what?" I chewed furiously on my bottom lip, then said, "I just hide on the breeding ship in your room and hope no one finds me?"

"No," he reached across the table. "I have already put in a request to take a transport ship back to the portal to Miez. We will travel back to Miez together and start a new life there."

As Korin spoke, describing the homes of the valley dwellers and how they did not use right angles in their architecture but mimicked shapes found in nature, my mind was suddenly flooded with rich, vibrant images of his world; the buildings, plants, and animals. Again, a clear image of the fern with the blue insect came into view in my mind's eye. It was overwhelming as if I had been seeing in black and white all my life and I was suddenly seeing brilliant colors that I never knew existed.

For weeks, I had been confronting the life I was leaving behind, and this was the first moment I really grasped the scope of the life ahead of me. My future - our future - was filled with uncertainty, but also adventure and discovery. I would be the first of my kind to experience a world that no one else had ever dreamed of. And Korin, he would be there with me, looking at me as if I was the most beautiful creature he had ever seen.

"Are you making me see things?" I asked.

"Can you see it?" he got up and walked around the table to kneel beside me and took my hand.

"I've never felt anything like it," I exhaled, and a tear rolled down my cheek. "It's beautiful."

Caught up in the intensity of the moment, I leaned forward and kissed him. As soon as our lips touched, something amazing happened. I saw myself as Korin saw me. Not just as I was now. I saw his first memory of me and everything he felt as he studied my life.

My incubation was his assignment. His performance would determine if he was qualified to work on the Earth's surface. But early on in the process, he had developed empathy for me and, as I approached the end of my incubation period, he knew he wouldn't be able to go through with it. He was going to fake my death and give up his dream job to save my life.

As I saw myself through his eyes and felt what he felt, for the first time in my life, I saw myself as something exquisite and beautiful. As human beings, we trust that we are loved and that the person we are with believes we are beautiful. But taking such things on faith is very different from experiencing love for ourselves through their eyes. I didn't just believe… I *knew* that he loved me.

He lifted me up and I wrapped my legs around his waist as he laid me down on the couch. He pulled my pajama pants off and I sat up and pulled his shirt over his head, tossing it onto the floor. I pulled him down to a seated position on the couch, throwing my leg over him as I straddled him. His hand slid up my thigh, his fingers grasping my panties that still clung to my hips.

He grabbed my hips and pulled me away from him to make eye contact.

"Stop," he whispered.

"Why?" I breathed.

"You're sensing what I want," he said weakly and touched my face. "This isn't what you want."

"Yes, it is," I tried to kiss him, but he turned away. "I don't know how to make you see what I see or feel what I feel, but it's there."

"If that's true, we'll have plenty of time for this," he said and kissed my cheek. "I won't risk taking advantage of you being overwhelmed with my feelings. Being loved and loving someone is not the same thing."

"I don't understand," I said meekly. Tears filled my eyes and my throat tightened.

"You are in a vulnerable place and it would be unethical for me to take advantage of you in this state. My kind have trained ourselves for centuries to disconnect from the emotional aspect of telepathy. For us, it is only images and information. I can sense that for you it is different," he said, then kissed my cheek and moved me aside. "I am going to go to work. I will be back in about ten hours and we can begin another session. After it is done, I am going to run a complete diagnostic to see if another session is even necessary. At the rate you are changing, one session might be all that is needed."

I nodded, pressing my lips together. I wanted to do for him what he had done for me. I wanted him to see and feel everything that I felt for him. But I didn't know how.

Chapter

THIRTEEN

Korin had been gone for about two hours when I heard my phone go off. Of course, it was Nathan.

*What are you doing tonight?*

I rolled my eyes. *I've got plans…* I responded.

*Who's the guy that's been at your place the last couple days?*

I squinted at my screen, thinking he was probably bluffing. *What are you talking about?*

*The guy with the dark hair that dresses like a Bernard & Thomas model.*

My blood ran cold. Bernard and Thomas was a clothing brand that typically signed tall, lean, male models. For all I knew, the clothes that he had purchased had probably come from a B&T store. The fact that he had obviously seen Korin wouldn't have been so alarming, except for the fact that Korin was only ever inside my house.

Either Nathan was outside looking through my windows or he had left some kind of surveillance device in my house. It wasn't like that kind of equipment was hard to come by these days. You could get tiny cameras to attach to your clothing or just about anything for no more than a day's wages for an average person. I looked at Nathan's fedora that was sitting on the mantle above my fireplace. I grabbed it and tossed it into the fireplace before dousing it with paint thinner and throwing in a lit match. I watched it go up in flames and opened the flue to suck the smoke out through the chimney. I couldn't remember the last time I had used my fireplace, but I was sure it had never been more useful than it was at that moment.

*I bet your wife might actually fuck you if you paid half as much attention to her as you do to your exes.*

That was the last text I would send Nathan before blocking his number. I was literally less than 24 hours away from leaving my life behind forever. The last thing I needed was a psycho stalker ex-boyfriend.

I sat down to write the first of three handwritten letters. The first was for Laura.

*Dear Laura,*

*I'm sorry for being such a shitty friend...*

I crumpled the paper in my hand and tossed it into the wastebasket. Starting over, I took a deep breath and spent a few seconds thinking about what the last thing I would ever say to her would be.

*Laura,*

*My beautiful, amazing, once in a lifetime best friend. I want to thank you for always being there for me. Thank you for breaking into my house when I was passed out on the floor. Thank you for forcing me to go out to the movies when I really wanted to stay home and practice origami. But most of all, I want to thank you for loving me when I was too low to love myself, for finding the good in me, and believing that I was worthy of your love.*

I stopped writing for a moment and wiped my eyes.

*I'm sorry for missing out on so much these last few weeks. I wish I could promise that I'll stop being flakey. I wish more than anything that I could have been there to see Alex propose. I wish I could be there at your wedding and stand beside you, holding your hand while your babies are being born. I know that you'd be right there for me.*

I sniffed and cleared my throat.

*The truth is, I don't know what my future holds. I've learned that my life is a very uncertain thing, and everything seems to change one minute to the next. I may miss many more special moments in your life, but I need you to know that it's not because I don't love you.*

*You've been the single most solid tether to my humanity, and I want you to know that I wish I could spend my whole life trying to repay you for everything you've done for me.*

*I wish you all the love and happiness that I'm sure is in store for you and I want you to know that I'll never forget you, as long as I live.*

*Love you always,*

*Nattie*

I wrote two more letters; one to my mother and one to Abiola. I wouldn't put them in my outgoing mailbox until it was time for me to leave. I knew I couldn't say a formal goodbye. So, I just told them how much I loved them and appreciated everything they had done for me over the years. I told them how sorry I was for every time I was emotionally walled off from their attempts to connect with me. And I told them how sorry I was for all the ways I failed as a daughter and a friend. I ended saying that they would never know exactly what they meant to me, but that I hoped they knew it was a great deal more than I was capable of expressing.

When Korin had given me the chance to see myself as someone who was worthy of love, my heart had begun to heal, and I could offer apologies without a sense of shame or pain. Through his eyes, I had come to realize that I had been broken and incapable of loving others past a certain point, and it was all due to my inability to love myself. But I was evolving past that and I could feel myself becoming more open to deeper thoughts and feelings than I had ever experienced.

When Korin came back, we went through the motions of cycling my blood and baking me under the lights. As I lay there, I found myself concentrating on Korin. I had never been very good at articulating what I was feeling, and I wondered if communication through images and feelings would be something that came naturally to me. I was a creature that had begun life as this profoundly emotional being that was now blossoming into an entity capable of expressing those images, thoughts, and feelings in their rawest form. It felt potent and dangerous in a delicious sort of way that I couldn't fully articulate.

I focused my intentions, recalling certain key memories; how I felt during the time we had spent together, the first time I ran my fingertips down the muscles of his arm as he slept, the way his nebulous eyes drew me in and made me feel like I was painting the birth of the universe. All the fear and distrust from years of disappointment and neglect that melted away every time he touched me. As I formed a series of images, moments, and the emotions attached to them, I took a deep breath and searched for his consciousness, a frequency that I could almost see. I matched the vibration of my own consciousness to his and sent out the message like a shockwave.

He flinched as it passed through him and he clutched his chest as if he was in pain. He looked at me through the glass, breathing hard as he placed his hand on the glass. I reached up and placed my hand to where his was. His eyes glistened with tears and he left the room.

What had I done? Had I pushed beyond some sort of boundary that I shouldn't have crossed? In a few minutes, it was time for the session to end and Korin returned, composed and ready to deal with the task at hand.

He disconnected me from the pump, allowing for the last of my blood to reenter my body before he took out the final tube and shut it down. He had me sit in the armchair and used some sort of hand scanner to go over my entire body.

"The infusion is complete," he announced and smiled widely. "All that is left is the neuron-alteration. We can leave as soon as you are ready."

My heart rate sped up at the thought of actually going through with leaving.

"I'd like to shower first. Would that be okay?"

"Of course," he nodded. "We are ahead of schedule. The chances of you making it home before giving birth are quite high."

I wondered if he was going to address the images that I had sent to him. There was no doubt in my mind that he saw and felt everything that was in my heart. I went to my bathroom and stepped into the shower, which was separate from my tub. The shower was completely enclosed with a door that swung outward. I turned on the water and waited for it to warm up. I could feel his presence in my bedroom, I even saw a small flash of him laying a garment out on the bed.

As I stepped into the steaming shower, I remembered him saying explicitly that his species couldn't read minds, but that it was a deliberate form of communication. I couldn't help but think that I was overstepping and trespassing in his mind somehow. Was my human intuition combining with the evolution of my newly developed psychic abilities and giving me an advantage that neither human nor Miezen people possessed?

My entire being, mind, body, and spirit (if there was such a thing), were all aligned and ablaze with new senses that I didn't understand, and every one of them craved him on every level of my existence. I closed my eyes called out to him in my mind, my hands moving over the curves of my body wishing he was there with me. He felt my call... I sensed him moving towards the bathroom before hearing the door open and feeling the cool air swirl in with the steam as he opened the shower door.

I opened my eyes and went to him, helping him undress before pulling him into the shower with me. His skin glistened as the water ran over it and I savored the cool sensation of his skin against me as he backed me against the shower wall and pressed his body into me. I put my arms around his neck, and he held one of my thighs up pulling me close.

I sighed. I had been so angry at him for so long. But now I finally understood; I knew, not just believed, that he would never intentionally hurt me. Just as he knew that I forgave him, and everything would be different after this. Our connection was such that any guesswork was eliminated and there was complete and transparent honesty between us. There was no room for misunderstanding or insecurity. Everything was known and it was beautiful.

He filled me completely; not only with his body but also his consciousness. It was then that I realized what I had always perceived as a soul could be accessed through the mind. The mind is not merely contained in the fleshy organ that is our brain. The soul and the mind are intertwined and this is the part of every living creature that craved a physical existence through which to experience the world.

I moaned loudly as we moved together, him thrusting against me, pinning me against the cool shower wall. I could feel every sensation on another level as I connected with his mind. I felt what he felt, and he was completely attuned to anything and everything I wanted. His hands slid over my body as he worked himself in over and over, all the while pouring into my mind, his vision of our humble but beautiful future together. This baby would only be the first of our family and while we would spend our days in a home nestled in a secluded valley-village, our family would know love beyond the imaginings of any other living creature.

The psychic friction between our bodies felt electric, our minds synchronizing as the rhythm intensified and we shared the most mind-shattering orgasm I'd ever had.

We spent the rest of the shower washing the sweat and sex off of each other. I stole kisses whenever I pleased. Afterward, when I dried off, I found the dress he had laid out on my bed. It was beautiful, with ornate silver embroidery adorning the purple fabric.

"It's what Miezen women wear in the days following a new marriage."

"Are we married?" I held it up, inspecting it.

"We didn't get the luxury of a ceremony," he said, leaning against the door jam. Beads of water were still dripping from the tips of his hair. "But the digital documentation attached to your identity indicates that we did just marry."

"I would marry you if I could," I smiled.

"I know," he grinned back, and in that moment, I felt how much he loved me once again.

I rushed and put my letters to Mom, Laura, and Abiola in my outgoing mailbox. I held the letters at the edge of the slot as I held my breath. *Forgive me.* I exhaled heavily and pushed the letters in. It was done.

It took Korin two trips to return all the stolen equipment, but when he was done, it was time for us to go. I walked outside to my back patio and looked out over my yard, inhaling the familiar scent of rain as the first few drops began to fall. Surely this was the last time I would ever smell it. I didn't say it out loud, but I felt it. I said goodbye to the world that I knew; a world that had held so much pain but also so much more love and light than I had realized until that moment. Walking back inside, I took a final look around my house. I nodded and Korin came close, brushing his cheek against my forehead. When he took my hands in his, I could feel the travel-ore in his hand. Together we moved up through the ceiling and out through the atmosphere.

In seconds, we were standing in his bedroom.

"We must hurry," he said. "The shuttle bay will be closing for this cycle and we will have to wait another 12 hours if we miss this one."

There was some more stolen equipment in Korin's apartment - a sort of helmet sitting on the floor in the corner. It was attached by several cords to a two-foot tall pillar, which he dragged with some effort to sit beside his bed. I laid down on the bed and he helped get the helmet properly fitted to my head. As he turned the machine on, I felt a series of electrical popping sensations inside my skull. It was uncomfortable but relatively painless.

I had only been lying there for a few minutes when a tone sounded. Korin's eyes widened and I knew something was wrong.

"You must hide!" he whispered.

I felt extremely dizzy as soon as I sat up. He took my hand and helped me up before practically stuffing me under the bed. He moved the heavy little pillar toward the back of the bed and hurried out of the room. I heard the door whoosh open and a female Miezen speaking.

"Korin, I was disappointed to hear that you lost one of your incubators."

"Yes, it was most unfortunate."

"I understand things had been going well. This outcome was most unexpected."

"I agree."

"I understand your failure has prevented you from being promoted to the Surface Research Team."

"That is correct."

"I have submitted a request to my superiors to have you assigned to a new incubator. I feel that your skills surpass those of many senior officers on this ship. It would be a shame to let such potential go to waste when it is obvious that your incubator expired through no fault of your own."

"Your confidence is most appreciated, but I do not feel confident that I am qualified to work on the breeding program."

"It is not pleasant work," she said. "But it is important that we do not allow our weaknesses to affect our judgment, especially us doctors."

"I am aware of this. I thank you for putting in your request, but I have already scheduled transport back to the portal. I have made the decision to return to Miez and work as a physician for our own people."

"That is most peculiar. For one with such lofty aspirations, you should accept the probationary period and advance to the Surface Research Team."

"It is my desire to return home."

"I find that decision to be ill-advised and surprising, but it is not for me to force you to accept the opportunity."

"I thank you for the opportunity to work on your crew, Axis," Korin said.

"I thank you for your service to the breeding program, Korin. I wish you a safe journey home."

*The room is spinning.* I said to Korin through our telepathic link.

*Dizziness is normal,* he answered as he saw his supervisor to the door.

"Can you understand what I'm saying now?" He asked as he helped me out from under the bed.

"Yes," I answered, and his face lit up.

"I am speaking to you in a Miezen dialect," he said excitedly and kissed me. "It's finished!" We laughed and he held me close. "I need to return the stolen equipment."

"Let me help you," I insisted. I stood up and took a moment to get my balance.

"No," Korin shook his head. He took me by the hand and gestured for me to sit back down. "You need to rest for a few minutes. I will be right back."

He lifted the pillar, which seemed to cause him to strain, then disappeared through the door. A few minutes passed and I found myself looking at the mandala patterns of my fingerprints. My skin was soft and firm, and every inch of my body felt sculpted and toned. I looked out the window at the Earth and the sun beyond it. I noticed that my arms were completely smooth with not so much as a hint of peach fuzz. In fact, my entire body from the neck down was completely hairless. I tried occupying myself, noting all the subtle ways my body had changed, but after Korin was gone for almost an hour, there came an announcement over a loud-speaker.

"All physicians to the medical bay. Repeat, we have a medical emergency in the medical bay. All physicians must report immediately."

*What's going on?* I asked in my mind, reaching out to Korin's frequency.

*There was an accident on a passing ship. They have docked here to receive emergency medical care for their crew. I will have to request special permission to leave.*

Time passed. I sat on the bed wringing my hands until he finally burst through the door wearing his lab coat. He held a second lab coat draped over his arm.

"Put this on," he said, handing it to me. I did as he said. "There is still time to get our shuttle. Our transfers are being approved. Your name is Ren and you work as a custodian here on the E-Orbiter-3,"

"You mean I clean up all the blood and guts?"

"Essentially," he shrugged. "We have just been married and we are going home to Miez to raise our family there."

"Okay," I nodded with a nervous smile. "Let's go home."

Hand in hand, we made our way down the corridor in the opposite direction of the operating room I had seen before. We passed a few other Miezen doctors, all with the same sharp features and various skin tones. Their expressions were so severe, and none of them were quite as attractive as Korin. I tried to avoid eye contact and not make a spectacle of myself. I realized with a brief flash of amusement that, in many ways, this was not so different from any other time I ventured outside my house.

"Korin," a voice called out behind us. We turned to see another doctor walking toward us. He looked familiar but I couldn't remember where I had seen him. "I was informed that you are leaving us today."

"Yes, Rodus. I am returning to Miez by shuttle in a few minutes, as long as we are able to get there in time."

"Is this your wife?" the doctor asked and eyed me closely.

"Yes, this is Ren," Korin replied and put his hand on the small of my back. "Ren, this is Rodus. He is a senior officer on the breeding program."

"Hello," I said flatly trying to mimic the way they spoke to each other.

"It is odd that a doctor would marry a custodian. You worked hard to receive your title and station to simply marry and return home with nothing."

"I have re-evaluated my priorities," Korin said, stiffening his posture.

"Interesting," said Rodus. "I hope you have a safe journey. I congratulate you on your recent marriage."

With that, he walked away and Korin and I continued on.

"What's up his ass?" I whispered.

"He was being intentionally rude due to the fact that our supervising officer wanted me to replace him."

"I see."

"He is a dick," Korin looked at me and I saw a hint of a smile pass over his face. I smiled and looked down, trying to recompose myself in case we ran into anyone else between here and the portal.

*Just relax your face and clear your mind,* Korin's thoughts came to me. *I have struggled to control my own emotions for years. I know you can do it.*

We reached the shuttle bay where Korin and I approached a female Miezen who stood in front of the gate door. Flares of light flashed behind her and noises gently rattled the gate. Korin squeezed my hand and I took a breath for courage.

"Shuttle reservation for Korin and Ren," he stated coolly.

"You made it just in time," she said, looking at her tablet as she spoke. She gave the slightest of nods then opened the gate and placed a small button in Korin's hand, which he then clipped onto the collar of his uniform. She eyed me suspiciously. "Congratulations on your recent union."

"Thank you," Korin nodded and took me by the hand, leading me through the gate into the windy docking tunnel and toward our assigned sleek black shuttle.

It was about the size of a car, conical, and it hovered a few inches off the platform. As I caught a glimpse of my fiery red hair flap against my newly tinted skin, I couldn't help but nervously chuckle. I felt like I was part of a superhero movie. The top of the shuttle folded forward and Korin quietly showed me how to climb in. Soon he was in the seat beside me and the clear conical dome folded toward us, sealing us inside. I felt myself relax a little, realizing that we would be off this disgusting ship in a few moments.

"I'm scared," I said, trying to keep my composure as he handed me a helmet. The large countdown clock by the bay doors didn't help my anxiety either.

"I know," he said and reached over to squeeze my hand. "But you do not need to be afraid."

We put our helmets on and it seemed to create a vacuum seal around my neck. As the clock flashed 00:01, he took hold of the shuttle controls and the bay doors opened, allowing us to speed out into the star-filled sky. Moments later, I looked out and saw my beloved Earth, slightly misshapen and more gray than blue. This was a memory I knew I would treasure for the rest of my life; my home planet suspended in the midst of an endless void.

In the distant future, human beings would be a thing of the past. Although I couldn't help but think how resilient our species has always been. After all, we have survived massive meteoric impacts, nuclear winter, and an ice age. We coexisted with dinosaurs, for crying out loud. Perhaps we, like the carnivorous trees on Miez, would find a way to keep coming back.

Earth grew smaller in the background as we sped through the cosmos. The portal was a million miles away and, according to Korin, the journey would only last just over an hour. I felt like I was in a dream. Korin put his hand on my thigh and we locked eyes, sharing mental images of everything that we hoped would await us on Miez. For the first time since leaving Earth, I felt elated at the thought of setting foot on my new home planet.

"Are you okay?" Korin ventured.

"I think I feel better than I've felt in a long time."

"You were always beautiful, but I cannot deny that your new species becomes you. By Miezen standards, you are positively stunning."

"Are you hitting on me, doctor?" I asked teasingly.

Everything went dark for a moment as we entered the cloaked portal station. Korin explained that what looked like an empty void at first was actually a bustling facility floating amidst an organized chaos of moving vehicles.

"What do you think?" Korin asked. I looked around us in awe at all the different ships gathered at the port.

"It's amazing," I breathed.

Our ship got into a queue to wait for our turn to pass through a brilliant giant spinning ring that hung at the center of the station.

A figure in a spacesuit drifted slowly in front of us, holding up its hands as if asking us to halt. The suit seemed to be propelled with small air rockets that attached at the wrists, ankles, and waist. A voice spoke over the intercom inside our shuttle.

"What is your point of origin?"

"The E-Orbiter-3," Korin answered.

"What is your destination?"

"Miez."

"Do you have clearance to leave your post?"

"Yes."

"Does your passenger have clearance?"

"Yes," Korin answered again. "We have a marital contract."

"Please wait while we verify your information," the attendant ordered, hovering in front of us.

I could feel myself hyperventilating. Neither Korin nor I spoke a word or even looked at one another. Rather, I focused on looking at the controls of the ship, counting the buttons and trying to distract myself from the urge to panic.

"Proceed," the attendant finally said and moved aside to allow us to pass.

I breathed a sigh of relief. I had always been in a constant state of preparing myself for the worst-case scenario. If I always expected the worst, I figured I'd never be disappointed. I made a decision at that moment to try and be a more optimistic version of myself. This was the perfect opportunity to start over and let go of the hang-ups that had previously kept me from living life to the fullest. I saw a bright purple flash as the shuttle at the front of the queue passed through the portal.

"Jeez! That what epic!" I exclaimed and squeezed Korin's hand.

"Wait until we get to the other side," Korin smirked.

There were only three shuttles ahead of us when the attendant returned with six other figures in identical suits. They covered our field of vision and the voice came through the intercom again.

"Halt, Korin. You are under arrest!"

Korin's breathing changed. He looked at me with desperation in his eyes before shifting his gaze back at the dark faceless figures looking at us from their tinted helmets. Ignoring their warning, he pulled back on the controls and rose the shuttle over the tops of the others, pushing forward toward the portal.

"Halt, or we will use force!" The attendant persisted.

Korin continued pushing against the seven suited attendants that were holding our shuttle and slowing our pace to a crawl. I looked at Korin and saw an expression of anxiety that made me realize that we had lost. One attendant produced a small device that stuck to our windshield. It beeped three times before detonating and cracking the dome on our shuttle. Our helmets would continue providing us with breathable oxygen but as the air escaped the cockpit of our shuttle, I also felt the artificial gravity give way.

I screamed as they pounded on the glass with their fists, breaking the barrier away piece by piece and pulling us from our seats. Several other vessels twice the size of our little shuttle pulled up and placed themselves between us and the portal.

As they pulled Korin in one direction and me the other, they shut off our com-devices and I knew he couldn't hear me just as I couldn't hear him. I could see his mouth moving and I felt him in my mind.

*I will find you.*

His voice echoed in my head.

*I promise.*

# Chapter

## FOURTEEN

One of the officers that grabbed me plugged a vial into my helmet and I heard a sharp hiss just before my vision faded. I felt as though my awareness was suddenly limited to the life force that powered my body. I knew I was being moved but I couldn't see, feel, or hear anything. I was simply somehow aware that I was going back in the direction we had come. I could sense Korin too. He was being taken somewhere else, somewhere far away. Suddenly there was a cold imposing darkness that barred my frequency from finding his. His consciousness faded from my mind and I felt myself losing consciousness.

When my eyes finally fluttered open, I found myself in the back of a car. The seats weren't cushioned like a normal car. They were made of smooth hard plastic with no seatbelts, as if to allow for easy cleanup should someone vomit, or bleed, all over it. There was some sort of reinforced glass shield between the back seat and the cab of the vehicle. I put my hand on the passenger side window. It wasn't regular glass. This seemed like something cops would use to move a serial killer.

I knocked on the bulletproof barrier and talked to the driver and his partner that sat in the front seat.

"Sit back and relax, Winters," the man in the passenger seat called over his shoulder. His voice was muffled by the glass, but I could still hear him clearly.

"Huh? Where am I?" I weakly pounded on the glass with my fist. "Who the fuck are you?"

"There is no need to be alarmed. You are safe now," he turned and took off his dark sunglasses to look at me. "You are under the protection of the SSC and we are not going to let anything bad happen to you."

"What the hell is the SSC?" I shrieked. My heart rate rose as the sedative wore off.

"The Secret Space Confederation," he stated bluntly, if not a little proudly. He picked up his radio and spoke into it, and I could hear his voice over an intercom speaker. "Your boyfriend is on the line. I am going to patch him through."

*Korin?* My head jerked up.

"Hey Nattie," Nathan's voice came through the speaker. "I don't know what the fuck you were thinking. You've always been a hardheaded woman, but I never thought you were stupid. You're lucky you happened to have a well-connected boyfriend like me. I was able to alert the proper authorities and get you out of there before it was too late."

My blood came to a sudden boil. He was the reason we had been stopped. I kicked the seat in front of me and screamed. I wanted to scratch the shit out of his face. There were no words for how much I wanted to rip him apart. How was it possible that Nathan of all people was involved in some secret space agency? The fact that no one really knew what he did for a living had made me think he was shady like he was laundering money or something; not that he was part of a government agency that was aware of the existence of aliens.

"We'll talk soon. Kisses..." he said and then there was silence.

I suddenly felt the cold reality of what was happening set in and soak all the way through my bones. Obviously, there was a lot that I didn't know, but I would get to the bottom of it somehow. The rain I thought I had left behind pattered against the bulletproof windows and a sense of dread crept in. Something inside me knew that the worst was yet to come and the fear of what that meant left me feeling paralyzed and hopeless.

We reached an underground tunnel where we drove for what felt like a couple of hours. I thought about Korin and wondered where he was and what they were doing to him. I rubbed my face with my hands, trying to stay calm. The feeling of my skin was so different.

*So close... We came so close! We would have been happy together, I think. It's hard to imagine but I know I would have been happy. Where have they taken him? Are they hurting him?*

I clenched my jaw at the thought. The old Natalia would have been a sobbing mess, but my skin wasn't the only thing that had changed. I felt stronger and more capable than I had ever felt in my life. The people that were trying to take possession of me didn't know what I was capable of and neither did I. All I knew was that I felt a cold clarity that made me feel powerful and dangerous in spite of the fact that I was caged.

The car slowed and came to a stop in the middle of the tunnel. The two men got out and stood side by side as they opened the door beside me. They stood poised as if ready to take me down if I tried to fight or run away. I didn't... I complied and let them pull me to my feet and walk to a door that was the same color as the rest of the tunnel. Even the door handle was the same dull gray. They must have used a sophisticated GPS to find it because it was hard to see, even if you knew what you were looking for.

They left the car and walked me through a corridor that opened up into a lobby. An attractive natural red-haired receptionist was sitting at a window; more bulletproof glass.

"Is this Miss Winters?" she looked up.

"Affirmative," the agent on my left stated.

"Please sign here," she pushed a document toward him, and he signed it.

I heard a familiar voice and I peered behind her to see Nathan, sharply dressed, standing there pointing at something out of view. He was standing tall and confident, his posture completely different from the cowardly weasel I was used to. He was giving orders to a team of people, doling out assignments for something they were working on. This commanding authoritative version of him was just further evidence of how manipulative he really was.

*Does she recognize him?* The receptionist thought, looking me up and down. *Of course, she does. She has a vagina. He probably fucks her too. Why would Nate limit himself to human women?*

Unnerved at the realization that I not only heard the thoughts in her head but sensed the disgust and jealousy that came with it, I stared at her. Was I having a mental breakdown? Maybe the neuron alteration had fried something. The receptionist hit a button and two sliding doors opened, allowing us to enter yet another hallway. The fluorescent lights overhead buzzed, and I felt my abdomen tighten and the weight of something shift inside me.

*The baby knows that I'm afraid.* I don't know how I knew that but that was the thought that came to me. I tried to stay calm, assuring myself that everything was going to be alright. Concentrating, I could tell that the agent on my right was thinking about what he wanted to eat for dinner. The agent on my left was busy thinking about how much he was in love with the agent on my right and wished he wasn't so afraid to tell him so. They opened the door to some sort of interrogation room and gestured for me to sit down. I did so without displaying any attitude whatsoever. If I was going to somehow gain the upper hand, I needed to make them all feel at ease.

My belly shifted again, and I felt a mild downward pressure in my gut. The two agents left the room and I crossed my arms. It was as cold as a hospital in that room. I rubbed my hands together before putting them inside my lab coat to try and warm up. I felt a curious crinkle of something in the inner breast pocket. I held out the lapel of my coat and, looking in at the hidden pocket, I saw the corner of a piece of paper sticking out.

*That doesn't make sense*, I thought, reaching for the paper. *Miezens have a powerful distaste for paper documents.* As I pulled it out, I saw that it was a small envelope with a page of folded stationery inside. Carefully, I opened it and felt my throat instantly tighten as I read the words.

*My Dearest Natalia,*

*I know this world must seem strange to you. Your senses will be overwhelmed at first by the unfamiliar sights and sounds. But please don't be afraid, I will be here with you every step of the way. I hope you like the house I've chosen for us. As you can see, I've set aside a secret room where you can paint.*

*I have written you this letter because I want you to know that I love you. In spite of how you've changed, there is still a part of you that is very much human. Humans have a hard time believing that which is not right in front of them, so I offer you this.*

*Let this letter be tangible proof that you are loved. This will always be true and must never be forgotten. Should you ever doubt this, please look at this letter and remember that I would do anything for you. Even spend hours to make sure every word of this was written elegantly and thoughtfully because the feelings I hold in my heart are true.*

*Of all the beautiful things I have encountered in this vast universe, you are the masterpiece of the cosmos. And I will love you until the end of my days and beyond.*

*Sincerely,*

*Korin*

I remembered when we had talked about love letters. He thought they were demeaning and said that he could never imagine why anyone would go through the trouble to write one. But he did. How long, I wondered, did it take him to learn to write with perfect penmanship, incorporating swoops and flourishes on the words he found most emotionally relevant.

What was more, when I touched the paper, I could feel what he felt when writing it. I folded it and returned it to its hiding place.

Wherever Korin was, I had to go to him. The means and the opportunity may not have been afforded to me just yet. All I knew was that something inside me had transformed; something that neither Korin nor myself had anticipated when we completed the procedure. I had become something not yet encountered; not by the SSC, and not by the breeding program. Even I didn't yet know the full extent of my powers, but I did know one thing…

I would find the man I loved, and no force on this Earth or anywhere else would keep me from going to him.

**Alice Bane** holds a BSc and a voracious interest in all things extra-terrestrial. Self-identifying as a citizen of the universe, she has opted to travel the cosmos through her words. Million Miles Away is her debut Sci-Fi Romance novel.

Stay tuned for snippets from book 2 in the Million Miles series by subscribing @ www.alicebanebooks.com

Follow Alice on Instagram @alicebane_author

Made in the USA
Las Vegas, NV
24 October 2023